HOMECOMING

HOMECOMING

ELSA POSELL

HARCOURT BRACE JOVANOVICH, PUBLISHERS

San Diego   *New York*   *London*

Library of Congress Cataloging-in-Publication Data

Posell, Elsa Z.
Homecoming.

Summary: Their lives in a small Ukrainian town
dramatically changed by the 1917 Revolution,
the six Koshansky children and their mother
struggle to survive in an increasingly hostile
environment; after the mother's death,
the children escape to America.
1. Soviet Union—History—Revolution, 1917–1921—
Juvenile fiction. [1. Soviet Union—History—
Revolution, 1917–1921—Fiction.
2. Jews—Ukraine—Fiction] I. Title.
PZ7.P83817Ho   1987   [Fic]   87-7615
ISBN 0-15-235160-4

Designed by Sylvia Skefich
Printed in the United States of America
First American edition 1987
A B C D E

INTRODUCTION

This is the story of my family. We lived in the Ukraine in southern Russia where Papa worked for the official tsarist government. We were comfortable, happy, and secure. Then one day the picture of Tsar Nicholas was removed from its place of prominence in our house, and life for us became unbearable.

The year was 1917, and I was just a young child. Russia was in the midst of a war, and after three years of tremendous troop losses, shortage of food and starvation throughout the country, and revolutionary action in the cities, Tsar Nicholas was forced to abdicate. A provisional government was formed under Alexander Kerensky that lasted only six months, and the Bolshevik (Communist) government took control in October 1917 under Nikolai Lenin. Great turmoil followed as the armies of different political groups fought to take over the government. This period of civil war lasted for five years, until the Soviet armies were victorious in 1922.

I understood little of these politics. I only understood the upheaval and the changes in our own lives. Along with the wealthy, the nobility, and former government officials and workers, we, too, were now the enemies of the new Russia, to be stripped of personal property, arrested, searched, often beaten and shot.

Papa was lucky. Like many others, he was able to escape. Mama and her six children were left to face life in the most hostile environment. This story is based on our life during this most difficult time, our adventures, and our eventual escape to America.

Elsa Posell

HOMECOMING

MY LAST BIRTHDAY at home! I shall never forget it if I live to be a hundred. Lots and lots of presents from everybody and flowers from Papa, who bowed and kissed my hand as he gave them to me. Best of all was having Papa home. He had missed Vitya's last birthday.

Dinner was very special with all the food I loved best, and we were still at the table laughing and talking long after the red raspberry birthday cake was eaten and the long yellow candles were but stubs in their holders, flickering in small tired flames around the melted wax. We were all so happy!

When the clock struck nine, Papa suddenly pushed his chair aside. "Heavens, I had no idea it was so late. To your rooms, to bed!" He tried to sound gruff.

"Olya, I'll come soon to give you a good-night birthday kiss," Mama promised, and I followed Vera to the large square room we shared. She was almost two years younger than I and not much fun. I didn't want the day to end. I wanted to go on talking, looking at my presents, but she was asleep even before I started to get undressed. I envied Marina and Vitya, my two older sisters, who were whispering and laughing in their room next to ours.

✗ There were six of us children. Alexander, whom we called Sasha, was the youngest. With his black hair and blue eyes, he looked exactly like Lev, the oldest of us all, and both largely resembled Papa. Vera, with her velvet brown eyes and curly hair, looked like a smaller-sized twin of my sister Vitya, who was three years older than I. The beauty of the family was my eldest sister, Marina. With her waist-long, golden corn-colored hair and large violet-blue eyes, she looked as if she did not belong to us. I was the plain one in the family. My blue-green eyes were too large for my thin face, and my black hair pulled tightly into plaits did not please me at all, but our nurse, Parazka, told me that being good and obedient was more important than being pretty.

Our home was in Sudilkov, a lovely little town nestled between large apple and cherry orchards and sparkling delicate birch trees in the Ukraine in southern Russia. Only about a hundred families, all scattered in different directions, lived there.

We were one of the town's nineteen Jewish families. We lived in a large white house close to the beautiful church, but we went to the synagogue, a low whitewashed building where we gathered for religious services. It was a small building with only two rooms. The larger was the sanctuary, or prayer room, and the smaller was used for meetings and celebrations.

Mama came into our room that night just as I was getting into bed. She put her arms about me.

"This was the very best birthday ever!" I cried, and Mama hugged me.

"Now go to sleep, Olya. It has been a long happy day. Good night, big girl," she whispered. I fell asleep immediately, but something kept pulling at my sleep, and I sat up very suddenly, feeling frightened. Something was happening. There were voices, loud and angry, and I jumped out of bed. Sleepily I groped my way in the dimly lit hall toward the living room and there bumped into Lev, who had his arms about Mama. Marina and Vitya were leaning against the wall, their faces pale, troubled. I stood next to them, scared and wondering what was happening. We hardly heard Papa's voice, but the voice of the man with him was loud and angry. For a moment there was a brief silence, and then a voice that sounded familiar began to shout contemptuously.

"The Bolsheviks will deal with you. See to it that no one leaves this house. You are all under house arrest." Then the front door opened and shut with a bang. We rushed into the living room and found Papa slumped in his chair.

"Osip, who was it? It sounded like Constable Koznikov. How dare he come at this hour shouting at you?" said Mama.

"It was Koznikov, but he is no longer Constable Koznikov," Papa said softly.

"Then he dared come this late to ask for help to get his job back?" Mama asked.

"No, I wish that was it; then he wouldn't have shouted at me." Papa sounded distressed. "He is now Investigator Koznikov, and when I asked him what he was going to investigate, he pointed his finger at me and shouted that I was the first on his list."

"Why you?" Lev, my eldest brother, cried. "You have

always been kind to him, and Mama has helped his wife and children."

Papa put his hand over his eyes, shook his head, and said, "I am afraid things aren't going to be very pleasant for us."

Mama put her hand on his arm. "Osip, this affects the whole family. Tell us exactly what is going on."

"I really don't know too much—only what Koznikov said. He ordered us not to leave the house; we are all under house arrest and that . . ." He did not finish.

There was a knock at the door, and Grisha walked in. Without greeting us, he said, "Just by looking at you I know that Koznikov was here, and I wish I could say that everything will be fine." He cleared his throat. "I have some things to tell you, Osip Pavlovich. Would you like to talk to me alone or . . ." He looked at the rest of us. Mama spoke up.

"Grisha, the children already know. We were awakened by Koznikov's banging and shouting. All of us here ought to hear what you have to say." She looked at Papa, who nodded in agreement. Grisha waited briefly, trying to choose his words carefully.

"Things are bad, very bad. This morning the center of town was full of frenzied, hysterical people, shouting, 'Hooray for freedom, long live the Revolution, and to hell with the tsar.' "

"This is a natural reaction, Grisha. The last years of the war have been hard on everybody, especially on these poor peasants. Now with the tsar out of power, and the new government, they feel more hopeful. I do think that when the new regime is more firmly established, the people will come to their senses." Papa smiled. "Perhaps even Koznikov will come to his senses," he added.

"I wish I felt more hopeful. House arrest is only the beginning." Grisha stopped and looked at us hard. "We must be ready for the worst. All your property may be taken. You might even be sent to prison." Mother turned pale, and Papa jumped out of his chair and almost shouted. "Grisha, it's true I worked for the government. My father before me as well as other members of my family have worked for the Romanov tsars, but none of us ever did anything against the people. As Jews, we were useful if we were skilled, but we had no power whatsoever. Almost everyone in town is my friend." Papa stopped, out of breath, and seeing our frightened faces, said, "Let's not worry until we know more. In the meantime we will obey orders. We will stay in and not go out." He tried to sound more cheerful.

"I wish Parazka had been here. She will be the most upset when she learns that the children cannot have their exercise out of doors," Mama said. Parazka was a very important person in our lives. She had taken care of Mama when she was a child and came with her to Sudilkov when she married Papa.

Parazka knew each of us well and made sure we knew what she expected of us. She had eyes both in front and behind her, and nothing escaped her. She never changed. Though her face was wrinkled, the thick black plaits wrapped about her handsome head were those of a young woman. She dressed in bright-colored skirts with numerous petticoats, which swished as she walked, and the keys fastened to her belt on an enormous key ring jingled so that we could always hear her coming. We were sure she had a key for everything that locked in our house as well as one for every other lock in the town! We both loved and feared her.

Grisha and his beautiful, shy, soft-spoken wife, Dumka, were also part of our household. Grisha, who drove our carriage and made our garden beautiful, also found time to take us ice-skating or on long *droshky* rides. Dumka worked in the kitchen, cleaning, washing dishes, and helping our cook, whom Lev had named "the butcher" because we hardly ever saw her without a knife in her large red hands. We loved the people who worked for us and felt very close to them.

Parazka kept us all in the folds of her ample skirts, and we did not seem to mind. She worried and fussed over us the first days of our house arrest but tried to hide her concern from us. When Grisha told Papa in front of us that we were to expect trouble very soon, she scolded him.

"We will soon find out how they feel about me," Papa said loudly, trying to be brave. Grisha shook his head, an anxious expression on his face.

Then one day a rock was hurled at one of our living room windows. Fortunately, neither broken glass nor the rock came into the room because Grisha, expecting trouble, had closed the shutters tight. Father and Mother jumped up and gathered us around them. There were loud angry voices outside. Grisha dashed out of the room and returned with a vicious-looking pitchfork.

"What's that for?" Papa asked.

"Anyone who tries to get in here will have to face me with this," he answered solemnly. Mother turned pale.

"Surely you don't think they will try to get into the house," she whispered shakily.

"No one knows what they will do," Grisha said unhappily. "They really don't understand what has happened. They have gone wild, and—"

A furious banging interrupted him. He turned toward the door, but Papa stopped him.

"No, Grisha, it is my job to face whatever there is to face."

Papa opened the door. Men and women, including Koznikov, stood before us.

"Here, go right in," Koznikov shouted to the people behind him.

Father moved back, but before any of them could enter, Grisha appeared, with his shiny, sharpened pitchfork.

"Anyone coming into this house will feel this pitchfork in his belly," he said, holding it in front of him like a bayonet.

"Stupid peasant!" someone shouted. "Don't you know that you are free? You don't work for these people anymore. Let us in! Let us all share the fine things they have!"

Grisha did not move. Koznikov shouted something to the group behind him, and they turned one by one and started down the road.

"Dumb peasant! Put it down!" Koznikov ordered, pointing to the pitchfork. "I want to talk to Koshansky."

"Grisha, let him come in," Papa said.

Koznikov came into the living room and glared at us. "Send them out of here. I want to talk to you," he snarled at Papa. We started to follow Mama out of the room.

"Just the children! You stay!" Koznikov shouted at Mother.

We followed Grisha out of the room. As he passed Papa's chair, he said loudly, "I'll be right outside," and ushered us into the kitchen, where Dumka and Parazka were cleaning silver. We suddenly realized that they were as frightened as we.

Mother and Father were with Koznikov for a long time.

When he left and we finally were allowed to return to the living room, they looked ashen and weary. We sat silently until Grisha came to the door.

"There are two men to see you," he said, but before Papa had a chance to tell him to bring them in, two short, round, unshaven men, strangers, had pushed past Grisha and were in the living room.

"What do you want? What can I do for you?" Papa tried to be calm. They nudged each other, laughed.

"Nothing you can do for us! From now on, we will do all the talking and give all the orders," one of them said.

Pointing at Mama and Papa, the other shouted, "Get ready! You are to come with us!"

"What for? Where to?" Papa asked.

"For questioning," he replied.

Their coats on, Papa and Mama looked at us long and hard before they walked out. We had never before seen them ordered about by anyone, nor had we ever seen them so desperately troubled. As the door closed, we felt as though we were hanging on to a weak rafter ready to break at any moment.

2

HOURS LATER, WHEN they returned, they were disheveled, frightened, and very tired.

"What happened?" Marina cried. Neither Papa nor Mama answered her, and Parazka signaled for her to be quiet. She ushered us out of the room away from our parents.

Poor Papa! He looked as if he had not slept for weeks. We talked in whispers, and when Marina sat down at the piano, Parazka shouted, "No piano playing, and don't bother your parents; they have enough problems." In our distress, we began to wonder if Parazka, too, had joined the townspeople in hating us. Our anger toward her grew until we realized how troubled she, too, was, and that she tried to hide her fears by fussing at us. She scolded almost constantly. We were loud, too fidgety, wasted food, but her greatest worry was that we needed exercise and fresh air.

"You must get out for a breath of fresh air!" she clucked one day. "Vera, Marina, Lev, go out the back door and run through the trees, around the barn several times," she ordered. When I asked if Sasha and I could do the same, she frowned. "No, I don't think it would be safe." But she took us to play in the stable loft. We used to love the place, but somehow it had lost its joy for us, and we walked about woodenly, wondering when Parazka would tell us it was time to come in. But no sooner did we return to the house than we longed to go out again. As we watched through the shutter openings of one of the windows, we saw a man leave our house with a large metal pitcher in one hand and a pillow that Mother had embroidered in the other. Another man was struggling with a large quilt, which kept spilling all around him as he walked.

"Those are our things! Why are they taking them?" I whispered to Parazka angrily. She looked at me with such sadness in her face that I turned away, afraid she would burst into tears. We had never seen Parazka cry!

Several days later Vera and I were late for breakfast and when we came into the dining room, we were surprised to find Lev seated in Papa's place.

"Where is Papa?" we asked. Mother looked uncomfortable, and I purposely avoided Lev's hand signals to be quiet.

"Where is Papa?" I asked again.

"He had to go out of town suddenly," Mother replied in a toneless voice, but I persisted.

"Will he be back for dinner? When?"

Mother put her hands over her face and sat stiffly on the edge of her chair.

"I want Papa! I want Papa!" I began to scream.

Lev jumped from his chair, grabbed me by the shoulder, and shook me so hard that one of my hair ribbons flew off and landed across the table.

"Lev!" Mother shouted. "You are never to hurt the children." Lev returned to his chair, shaking with anger. My shoulder hurt and my face felt as if it were on fire. Mother reached across the table and took both my hands in hers. I did not dare look at her. I knew she felt miserable. Still, I could not stifle my wretchedness and anger, and as much as I wanted to throw my arms about her and cry, I could not do it. Instead I screamed, "You're not telling the truth!" and Mother slumped in her chair. I hurt so and was so full of rage that I hardly felt Lev's hand as it hit my left cheek. Again Mother cried out. "I don't want this to happen—ever again!" she told him sharply.

"She's a nuisance!" Lev pointed to me.

I looked at him angrily and screamed, "Did they get Papa?"

Mama bent over my chair and put her arms about me. "Olya, Papa is all right. I will tell you when I can. You *must* trust me," she said.

Later I found her seated at the large desk, feverishly pulling papers and documents out of drawers and handing them to Parazka, who quickly threw them into a large folder.

"All these must be burned!" Mama said, and Parazka immediately started to build a fire. I was surprised. This had always been Grisha's job.

"Where is Grisha?" I asked. Mother avoided my question.

"It's chilly, Olya, the fire will warm us up," she half mumbled. Rage again spilled over. Something was going on. Lev, Marina, and Vitya knew what was happening, and I hated them for not telling me.

"I'm old enough to know what's going on!" I shouted.

Mother raised her eyes, looked at me, started to say

something, and stopped. "You will have to trust me," she said quietly.

On the evening of the fourth day of Father's absence, we heard the clatter of horses and wagon wheels on the road.

"It must be Papa!" Vera and I cried excitedly, and rushed to the door.

Mother's voice was stern and loud. "Sit down and be quiet!" she said as she cautiously opened the door. It was Grisha. He was alone. Quickly he came in and Mother bolted the door behind him.

"Where is my father?" I cried tearfully, running up to Grisha, but Mother ordered me back to my chair. Grisha was rumpled, unshaven, and exhausted, and he ate hungrily the food Parazka brought to the table.

"What did you do with Papa?" Vera cried accusingly. "Why didn't he come back with you?"

Grisha, his mouth full of food, made no attempt to answer us. We watched him eat, trying to be patient, wondering if he would ever finish; but while he was still eating, Parazka appeared and took us to her room for a short time.

We rushed back to find Mother slumped in her chair, exhausted and pale. Grisha was gone, and Vera and I both cried, "Tell us about Papa!"

Mother looked at us in a frightened sort of way and whispered softly, "Father is out of the country."

This was nothing new to us; Papa had been out of the country many times. *Why does she sound so sad?* I wondered.

"Will he come back soon and bring us presents?" Vera asked.

Mother lowered her head and was silent.

"Don't ask so many questions!" Lev scolded, and turned

to Mother. "They are too young to understand." He gestured toward Vera and me.

Mother shook her head. "No, Lev. They, too, must be told. I will try to explain," she said. "Papa had to get out of the country. He had to escape quickly. Had he stayed, he would have been imprisoned or . . ." She stopped and swallowed hard. "Or even killed!" She spoke so softly that we could barely hear her. "I know it is hard for you to understand," she continued. "These are bad times for us. There is a revolution in our country. The tsar was overthrown. Different groups not happy with our present government are trying to organize their own. Some want the tsar back; others don't want him. One group fights another; it is terrible." Mother stopped and wiped her face with a handkerchief. "And we, because Papa worked for the government of the tsar, and because we live in this big house, are considered the enemy," she added, and stopped. "Why do I tell this to you? Lev is right. You are too young to understand. At least Father is safe; we must be thankful for that!"

"Will he come back?" Vera asked again, and Lev glared at her. Mother thought for a minute.

"I don't think so. Grisha risked his life to take him to the Polish border. From there, we hope he can get to America. When he does, he will send for us. Someday we will be with him again."

At the word *America*, Vera and I started to dance, chanting, "We're going to America! We're going to America!"

Mother clapped her hands angrily. "Stop it at once!" she cried. "This is a secret! We must never speak of this to anyone. Papa will be missed soon enough. No matter who asks, say you know nothing about him! He vanished!

We have no idea where he is. Don't ever, ever mention America!" she said sternly.

We were stunned. Father—gone! Where was he at this very minute? Had he started for America? Exciting, but so frightening! Was he really safe? What would happen to us? My thoughts were interrupted by loud voices outside and a pounding on our front door. We were too terrified to move. Mother and Lev exchanged looks of alarm.

"Stay as you are," Lev told us and went to the door. "Who is it?" he asked.

The only response was more banging. Lev hesitantly unlocked the door and three strange men pushed their way into the house.

"We want Koshansky!" they shouted. "Where is he?"

"When you knocked, we were hoping it might be someone with news of him," Mother cried. "He's been gone four days—no one has seen him. We are worried sick!"

"You lie! We don't believe you! We will find him!" one of the men shouted. Every room was searched; walls were tapped for secret doors. Mother was questioned, and when the men decided that they had done a thorough search, they demanded food. Mother took them into the kitchen and placed stew, bread, cheese, jam, and a pot of *borscht* on the table. Ignoring the forks and spoons, they stuck their fingers into bowls and licked them. They took turns drinking *borscht* out of the pot, spilling bits of cabbage, beet, and meat over themselves and over Parazka's clean floor. They could not have been very hungry for they just tasted the food and walked out.

The next morning as Parazka was serving breakfast, they returned. This time Grisha was with them. Parazka immediately took Sasha and Vera and disappeared with them to her room. A soldier followed her.

"If Koshansky is in your room, you will pay for this, old *babushka!*" he shouted. He looked under the beds, in closets, behind curtains and then left. The other two remained, shouting for us to tell them where Papa was. We clung to Mother and to each other, frightened, and watched them search the house, scream at Grisha, and threaten Mother.

"You'd better tell us; you must know where Koshansky is!" a soldier shouted, looking at Grisha.

"How would I know? He just disappeared; none of us here has any idea where he is," Grisha shouted back at him. The soldier turned to Mother.

"You'd better tell us, or—" and Grisha jumped in front of her.

"You idiot! Still protecting them," the soldier jeered. "Take what you want, throw these people out, move in here yourself." Grisha's mouth twisted but he remained silent and stood watching them open drawers, throw the contents on the floor, and stuff our things into their pockets.

Vitya, seeing her small box that contained the things she called her treasures, cried, "That's mine! Give it back!" The soldier took it out of his pocket, looked at it, and laughed.

"There must be something good in it if you want it." He kept it in his hand. Vitya lunged forward to grab it, and he raised his fist to strike her, but Grisha quickly pulled her back, and both men stood glaring at one another, ready to fight. Vera and Sasha began to cry loudly and ran to Grisha.

"You slow-witted peasant!" the soldier spat at Grisha and walked out. Mother was in tears.

"I am so sorry that you have to take all this abuse because of us," she said.

Grisha grinned at her in a tired way. "They don't bother me. I will help all I can," he told her. Grisha stayed with us the rest of the afternoon, and we realized how much we depended on him and how much safer we felt in his presence. Nothing seemed quite so bad when he was with us, and we could better tolerate the days in the darkened house.

Papa had been gone less than a week and daily his absence became more real and painful. We kept looking out through the cracks of the closed shutters, wondering what it was like outside. What changes had April brought to our trees and shrubs? How we wanted to go out! It seemed that we had been inside forever, but Grisha insisted that it was not safe to go out. We had to stay in and we obeyed, but there were temper outbursts, tears, and fights between the younger children. All of a sudden, there was nothing for us to do. The books we so loved stayed closed. Alone, when no one was screaming or threatening us, the house was strangely quiet, a quiet that clung to us like a net, and we felt trapped in it.

Daily someone banged at the door, looking for Papa, threatening, hurling insults at Grisha because he was helping us. It was therefore no surprise to us when after a particularly loud prolonged knocking, Grisha opened the door to two men who noisily entered the room. One wore the tunic of a soldier's uniform; the other wore no uniform. They walked into the living room and stared at us.

"Is this your house?" one of them asked Grisha.

"It is the family house of Madame Koshanska," he replied. They looked at Mother.

"The Bolsheviks have taken this town. We want this house for our headquarters," he said.

We were immediately relieved; it had nothing to do with Papa.

"But where is the family to live?" Grisha cried.

The soldier's eyes traveled around the room, rested on our faces. "That's not our problem; but there is a house at the back. We will let them live there," he answered.

"But my wife and I live in that house," Grisha cried in alarm.

The soldiers looked at him suspiciously. "Why do you live there?" they wanted to know.

"Because we work here," Grisha told them.

The soldiers looked at him in disbelief. "Don't you know anything? You are stupid. The Bolshevik Revolution has made you free; you are better than these . . ." He didn't finish.

Grisha's jaw was set and he looked straight ahead. One of the soldiers walked up to him.

"You idiot! You still don't know what's good for you? This is an order: you and your wife no longer work here. These parasites—" he pointed his arm in our direction— "will from now on do their own work!" Grisha was silently grim, and none of us dared look at him.

When Mother spoke, we were surprised at her calmness. "How soon will you need the house?"

"Tomorrow night. Take only what you must have," one of them said, and started making notes. "If you take too much we will come and take it back and throw you out," the other said as they walked out the door.

3

THE MINUTE THEY left, Grisha locked the door and turned to Mother. "Anna Nikolayevna, you know that neither Parazka, Dumka, nor I can work for you any longer. We must follow their orders, as you and the children must." He stopped briefly and looked at us. "You know we would never leave if we could stay."

Mother sat down very suddenly and put her head in her hands. Her body shook with sobs.

Grisha watched her for a second, shaking his head. "Don't worry about us," he said. "Parazka has her own cottage to go to; Dumka and I will live with my parents on their farm. You and the children must move into the cottage where Dumka and I live now. It is small but we must make the best of things."

Mother lifted her head, making no effort to dry her tear-streaked face. "You are right, Grisha. It is the only thing we can do," she said more hopefully.

"I must tell Dumka. We can pack today and move

tomorrow, but I'll be back in good time to move you into the little house," Grisha said.

"Not if it means danger for you. You have done enough for us," Mama told him. Grisha grinned at her.

"Anna Nikolayevna, I will move you all into the little house. Lev can help if that will make you feel better," he said firmly.

We spent the rest of the day in frenzied search for things we would need and could take to the cottage. Parazka made a list: warm clothing, shoes, coats, feather quilts, and other warm blankets. We were not to take many toys because there was no room for them in the cottage, but we were not limited as to the books we could choose. This made me very happy. I had so many favorites!

There was little conversation during dinner; we were each involved with our own concerns and thoughts. We knew the cottage well, having been there so often to visit Grisha and Dumka. It was a lovely little house, but now that we were to live in it, it quickly lost its charm. We knew it was too small for a family the size of ours. I was probably the one least upset about moving from our house. For me, our house was horrible without Papa in it. The light that he brought to it had vanished with him, and I hoped to lessen the pain of missing him by getting away from the house.

By evening our things were packed, and we were in bed early. I fell asleep, thinking about the small cottage surrounded by cherry trees that was to become our home. It seemed that I had just fallen asleep when Parazka tugged at my feet.

"Up, Olya!" she cried. "And wake Vera." It was early. The sun was just coming up and I wanted to stay in bed, but I knew better. I got some of my clothes on and woke

Vera. As always, I had to help her put on her stockings, which made both of us late. Dumka was serving breakfast, a delicious hot grain gruel topped with milk and sugar. I was hungry and enjoyed every bite. Mother hardly ate, and I kept wishing she would eat because it was such a wonderful breakfast. It was over too soon, and Mother told us to gather the personal things we had chosen with her approval. Vera and I went to our room. It looked so different! Lev and Grisha had taken the mattresses and pillows to our new house and the beds were bare. Our room looked empty and cold. Vera burst into tears.

"Where will we sleep tonight?" she cried.

"In Grisha's cottage," I told her.

"I want to sleep in my own bed right here!" Vera clung to her bed, sobbing. Mother rushed in and put her arms about her.

While she was consoling her, I looked around our room and was suddenly so full of sadness that before I realized what I was doing, I had dashed down the stairs and out the back door into the garden. I blinked in the bright sun and swallowed gulps of fresh air. It was cold! Too cold to be out without a sweater or coat. I tried to get back into the house but the door through which I had made my escape was locked from the inside. I dashed around to the front door, but as I reached it, I saw men and women coming up the road leading to our house. Luckily, the front door was unbolted. I ran in so fast that I tripped over a chair. Grisha picked me up.

"What's the matter?" he asked anxiously.

"People coming up the road to the house!" I screamed.

Grisha locked the door and disappeared. When he returned, his large shiny pitchfork was in his hands. He called

Mother and spoke to her quietly, then walked out the front door. Soon we heard angry voices that grew louder.

"Let me go out to help Grisha," Lev pleaded with Mother, but she pushed him back.

"I am the one to go out and see what these people want," she told him, opening the door. Grisha was in front of it, holding his pitchfork toward the people, who were straining to get into the house.

"Let us in!" they screamed. "We have more right to the things in the house than she." They kept pointing at Mother.

His pitchfork raised, Grisha stood in front of her, paying no heed to demands or insults from the people.

Mother raised her hand and surprisingly the small crowd quietened.

"What is it that you want?" she asked calmly.

"We want everything you have in the house" was the cry.

"But it is to be used as army headquarters. When the soldiers are in the house, get their permission to take the things you want," she said firmly.

A tall old man took off his cap, slapped it against his knee, and yelled, "Listen to the grand lady! She wants us to get permission!"

There was a ripple of laughter, and the group moved closer to the door. Grisha stood firm, gripping the pitchfork in his hands. Grumbling, the group started back down the road. Grisha rested his pitchfork on the ground with a sigh, as if suddenly realizing how heavy it had been.

"I'll move the beds to the cottage now," he muttered, and walked into the house.

The angry voices of the people reverberated in our

ears long after they left. Grisha continued moving things as if nothing had happened, while the rest of us almost fell apart. We had never before experienced such open hatred. My stomach felt as if it were full of jagged glass. I was suffocating! I had to get outside, and again, without telling Mother, I slipped out of the house.

It was so quiet that I could hear the branches moving in the wind, rubbing against each other. The only other sound came at short intervals, the joyous sound of birds. I ran toward the stable, around the little house where we would be living, and the ache within me began to ease, draining out of me like water out of a leaky teakettle. I stopped and peered inside, through the low windows. All Dumka's and Grisha's belongings were gone. Except for our bedding piled on a sheet in one corner, the house was empty. The earthen floor, dark yellow, was covered with sheepskin rugs from our big house. I went from window to window looking in. Next I ran, touching trees, putting my arms about them and pressing my face against the cool, rough bark. On and on I ran from one tree to the next, unaware of my tears. Suddenly I felt Mother's arms about me, and I knew she was crying, too. She spoke not a word. We just stood there, my arms around the tree, hers about me. Finally, Mother touched my face gently.

"It's all right, Olya. Sometimes it is good to cry. Let's tell Grisha where to put our beds." I felt better. I took Mother's hand, and together we followed Grisha into the little house.

"Lev ought to have a bed of his own," Mother said, measuring the room with her teary eyes. "We need four beds. Lev's bed will be in the kitchen. Sasha will sleep with me; Vitya will share a bed with Marina." She looked at me. "You, Olya, will share one with Vera."

"Will our beds all fit in this room?" I asked.

"Yes," Mother said. "It will be cozy," she added, trying hard to smile.

I was grateful not to be asked to go with them when Mother and Grisha left. I walked and looked at things in the stable as if I had never seen them before. The horses were gone, and I stood at the entrance, lost in thought until I heard Mother calling me. Then, slowly, I started back toward the cottage, where I found everyone bustling about, and I tried to feel guilty because I had not been there to help but could not. By late afternoon the beds were ready, but tempers flared. We were so discouraged. There was so little space for our things. Parazka's appearance at the door with a large pot calmed us. Placing it on the *petchka*—the stove, used both for cooking and heating the house—she turned to us.

"What's wrong? You are all so upset!"

Mother pointed to the things piled on our beds; Parazka's eyes darted about the room.

"What about this?" She pointed to a large trunk in a corner we had missed. She also discovered shelves and a large wall board with hooks and hangers for coats and other clothing in the kitchen.

"I don't know how we would ever have managed without you," Mother said. Parazka's face was a mask, expressionless, quiet.

"Here comes Dumka to serve dinner," she said loudly, pointing to the window. We looked out and saw Dumka limping down the path with a basket, followed by Grisha carrying a snowshovel and some other tools. When we turned our eyes back to the room, Parazka was out of the house.

"She's strange," Lev said. "Here we are moving into

this little house and she did nothing to help." Lev sounded puzzled, angry.

"Stop! You don't know Parazka if you can say this about her," said Mother unhappily.

Dumka and Grisha walked in. "We have your supper and want to show you where cooking pots, dishes, and other things are," Grisha said. Dumka was already filling soup bowls and asked us to sit down. There were chairs for us all around the well-scrubbed wooden table. After Dumka had served us good beet *borscht* with thick slices of bread and hot tea, she and Grisha went back to our other house to get it ready for the soldiers. It felt strange having dinner in the tiny house, but we ate hungrily just the same.

As soon as we had finished, Mother said, "We must do things for ourselves now. The sooner, the better," and she started clearing the table, directing Marina and Vitya to wash the dishes.

When Dumka and Grisha returned, they had their coats on.

"Where is Parazka?" we asked. Grisha and Dumka looked at each other and were silent. Mother held out her arms to Dumka, who shyly returned her hug. We all ran to Dumka, and when I kissed her, her face was as wet as mine. Grisha kissed Mother's hand, and we almost knocked him down as we rushed at him to say good-bye. He picked up Sasha. "Be a good boy," he said. Dumka walked out of the house without looking back at any of us. Grisha stayed after she had closed the door, looking pained and sad.

"You must know that we are not leaving because we want to," he said in a husky voice.

We looked at him, trying hard not to break down.

"You are our family. We will help you as much as we

possibly can," he added. Still we said not a word, and Lev opened the door for him. "Don't worry about the cow. I will be passing to take our cows to pasture and I will take care of her," Grisha said. The door closed and he was gone.

No one spoke. We stood there as if we had suddenly lost the ability to move. The bright orange-yellow of the sun on one wall was growing more and more faint as night crept in. Mother recovered first; she lit the paraffin lamp and placed it on the table.

"It has been a long hard day for us all." She sighed. "We should go to bed early tonight." By the time the first stars appeared, we were in our beds, our first night away from our big house.

4

TEARS, FRUSTRATIONS, ANGER, hurt feelings, and sharp tempers filled the first week of life in our new home. Mother, Lev, and Marina tried to settle arguments and fights between the younger children, and we soon learned that we could not dispute either Marina's or Lev's authority. Mother was the most patient, Lev the most strict, and Marina the most sympathetic; but all were fair in dealing with us. As soon as we accepted the change and the responsibility of jobs to be done, things were better. Even Vera and Sasha had jobs. They had to sweep the ground around the door and they took their responsibility very seriously. My job was to keep the buckets in the kitchen filled with water from the well. Mother took me to the well and explained the dangers if I did not follow directions. Over and over again she showed me how to attach the bucket and use the crank properly. I had to practice lowering the bucket, filling it, and pulling the full bucket up. Satisfied that I could be trusted, Mother allowed me to go for water all by myself, and I was dependable most of the time.

Warmer weather, too, helped ease tensions in the crowded little house. It was wonderful to be out of doors. Slowly, the tree trunks shed their old winter clothes and waited patiently for the new spring garments to take their place. Branches, stretching to reach the weak spring sun, showed swelling knobs, soon to become buds. The pale green haze above the trees, with a touch of soft pink, was almost unreal, and our forced freedom from school, piano lessons, and other obligations allowed us to watch and witness the birth of spring. If only Father were with us! We so wanted him to share this miracle with us.

One morning we opened our door to find ourselves in the midst of such enchantment that we could only stare in silent wonder. All around us the cherry trees were in bloom! Our small world had blossomed into a pink fairyland. We ran from tree to tree like bees, stopping only to touch the blossoms and to smell them with the gentle lightness of bright-colored butterflies.

Something was taking shape within us—the something we had thought lost to us forever. We were again able to laugh, sing, and feel alive. The only ache that never left us even for a moment was that of missing and worrying about Papa.

For weeks we went through this wonderful metamorphosis, afraid we were dreaming, and would wake up suddenly to the selves we were when we first left our big house, but we were not dreaming. Our confidence and strength grew stronger; we were on our own feet and the ground under them was not trembling.

"We must have a vegetable garden or go hungry," Mother said one morning, and we cheered. It took days of digging, raking, and breaking up clumps of soil to smooth the earth. Sasha and Vera picked weeds and stones. It was hard work. Our hands grew calloused and we were bone weary, but no one complained. It was such a good tiredness. We slept well, and there were few disagreements or fights even between the younger children.

The morning Mother was to go to market for seeds, we cried, "What are we going to plant?"

Mother smiled. "Any vegetable seeds I can get," she answered. But when we saw her on her return, our spirits dropped. She looked so unhappy.

"No one will sell me seeds no matter how much money I offer them." She patted her purse.

"Do you mean that after all our work we can't have a garden?" Marina asked angrily.

"I hope not," Mother replied. "I have an idea that if I offer something in trade instead of money, we can get seeds." She brightened suddenly and ran toward the house and returned with a sheepskin rug over one arm and her short light blue cape over the other.

"No, not your cape!" we all cried. Mother smiled.

"We need food far more than the cape," she said. Covering both with some faded cloth, she again started down the back path to the market.

This time she returned with onion, radish, cucumber, bean, beet and even potato seeds. We could hardly believe our luck and again worked long hours to smooth the soil, measure straight rows, and dig holes in which to place our precious seeds. Lev cut the potatoes into sections according to Mother's directions and placed them carefully into the spaces Vitya dug for them. At last the seeds were at home in our soil and we cared for them carefully, lovingly. It took buckets and buckets of water to keep the garden moist, and Vitya and Marina took turns with me to carry water from the well. We were like expectant parents, watching and waiting for a sign of growth from our precious seeds. Finally, one morning we saw tiny pale-green sprouts of onion pushing through the earth. Next came lacy tops of carrots, weak and delicate, growing stronger even as we watched them. We were wild with joy. Somehow, the seeds coming to life brought greater purpose and hope to our own lives.

In mid-June, Mother picked the first green stalks of onions and the red-pink heads of the radishes. We roared with laughter when Vera picked an onion, and hardly shaking off the dirt, stuck it into her mouth. What feasts we had! How good radishes and green onions smothered in *smetana*, soured cream, tasted! We watched excitedly for vegetables to ripen, and each night we banqueted on something wonderful the garden had brought forth that day.

One morning as we were having breakfast, there was a knock at the door. "Maybe it's Grisha with the milk, there was no milk at the barn this morning," Lev said, and opened the door. It was not Grisha but two young men who stood there. They were not in uniform, and both were annoyed with Mother when she asked, "Who are you and what do you want?"

"You don't know who we are?" one of them cried. "We are the comrades living in the big house. Today we caught one of the men who used to work for you. He was milking your cow and left the milk at the stable door."

Mother turned pale. "What have you done to him?" She tried to control her anxiety.

"Nothing yet," he replied. "We took the milk but let the stupid fool go. He must learn that he no longer works for you." We silently sighed with relief. Grisha was safe!

"We'd better not catch him helping you again," the soldier added. He looked at the table and the bubbling *samovar* appraisingly. "You still have a *samovar?* And what a big one! You know, no one is allowed to help you. Do your own work! You should get down on your knees to thank us for letting you live here!" he shouted.

We were shaken by their visit but grateful Grisha was safe.

"I can milk the cow," Marina spoke up. "I watched Dumka do it many times."

"Good!" said Lev. "And I will take her to pasture and bring her back."

Mother smiled. "I am proud of all of you! You do your jobs well and the garden is the greatest proof of it," she said.

"And we will continue working, won't we?" Lev asked.

"We will!" we shouted. Mother put her finger to her mouth indicating we were too loud and we all stood still, smiling and laughing, proud of what we had done. We worked hard, had enough to eat, and found that the ability to grow much of the food we needed was a most satisfying reward.

Early one morning as we went to pick vegetables for the day, we were stunned to see our beautiful garden naked, ransacked, in disarray. We stared in disbelief. Gone were most of the onions, radishes, and carrots. Gone were the ripe beans we had saved for the day's meal. We stood looking, speechless. Mother was the first to recover.

"I suppose the rabbits must have arrived here before us," she said, trying to laugh, but we knew she did not believe her own words, and despite her efforts, her face displayed the misery she felt. Slowly we walked back to the house, empty-handed. By the time we sat down, tears were running down Mother's face, dropping soundlessly onto the table. Sasha, frightened by her tears, climbed onto Mother's lap and kissed her. She rocked him in her arms, still crying.

"We still have many vegetables which will soon be ripe. We will also plant others, but we must watch the garden at all times," Lev said determinedly.

"We'll catch the thief!" Marina said angrily.

Once again, we weeded and then planted more seeds. Even at night, Lev left his bed to look at the garden. New vegetables were coming up, others were getting ripe, but not enough at once to keep our bellies full. We were often hungry and continued our watch. Mornings we ran to the garden before we even built a fire for tea. The plants were there—safe! Finally, after what seemed an eternity, enough vegetables were ripe, and we again anticipated dinners that would not allow us to go to bed hungry. Lev and Marina picked beans; Mother, her hair flying about her face, smiled and pointed to the vegetables ready and those that would soon be ripe. It was wonderful to see her smiling as we walked back to the house with our earthly treasures. Happiness is contagious! Mother's pink, smiling face filled us with hope; things were going to be better for us again.

Mother even resumed school out on the soft grass, and it was during one of these sessions that we saw them— three young soldiers in uniform, walking toward us. Mother urged us to continue working while she greeted them. They did not return her greeting, but stood silently staring at us. We pretended to work, though our hearts were racing.

"What have you done with our vegetables?" they asked. We were startled.

"Your vegetables?" Mother asked. "That garden is our only source of food. We planted it, cared for it. Those vegetables belong to us." She looked unruffled, but we could discern fear in her voice.

"Nothing here belongs to you," one of the soldiers shouted. "You must share everything with us."

Mother's face was a picture of wretchedness as she sat biting her lip, fighting hard not to talk back to them.

"Get us the vegetables you picked today!" one of the men ordered.

Mother asked Lev to get them. They had been washed and placed in several separate bowls. The soldiers selected those they wanted, leaving only a few for us.

"You see? Now we all have vegetables," they said. "We will come daily for half of your milk and the vegetables you pick. If you cheat us, we will know, and you will be punished." The soldiers walked away, swinging a basket full of the vegetables that we had worked so hard to raise. Mother's face, so pink and content just hours before, now showed defeat.

"I should have put up a fight to keep them from taking our food!" Lev cried angrily.

"It would not have done a bit of good," Mother said.

"I'm going to get it back!" Lev shouted and started for the path the soldiers took, but Mother caught him by the arm.

"Don't be foolish! You can't win!"

Lev stopped and for a moment we watched him grind the dirt under his left foot. His shoulders sagged and his fists were clenched. Mother put her hand on his shoulder.

"We must keep our heads. We are no match for them." She made a gesture toward the big house. "Take Sasha and Vera to help you find branches for kindling. It's almost time for supper."

I watched Lev walk off, followed by Sasha and Vera,

and wondered why we needed more wood when there were piles of wood stacked high against two walls in the kitchen. However, when the three returned carrying some dry twigs, they were all in better spirits, and I realized how wise Mother was.

That night Mother was restless. She left her bed several times, and we could see the dim outline of her bent head at the table.

"You all right, Mama?" Marina whispered.

No answer. Then finally she said, "I'm fine," but there was a catch in her voice; she was crying.

5

IT WASN'T LIKE Mama to stay upset and angry for long, but the incident with the soldier from the big house was one she found difficult to shake off. Every so often, we heard her mumble to herself, "The impudence, the gall of him!" and we knew that sadness and anger clung to her like frost on an icy day. We saw it in her face and felt it in her voice.

Every time one of them came for the vegetables and milk, we fully expected her to scream or to strike him, but Mama only tightened her lips and acted as if he was not there. "Get the milk and vegetables, Lev," was all she would say.

One day an ungainly, tall, thin one came as we were doing our schoolwork on the grass.

"There's not much here," he said suspiciously, looking into our bowl.

"There's not much in our garden," Vitya told him. "Go to the garden and look for yourself."

The soldier looked at her angrily. "I will, but I will also look in the house! I'm sure you're hiding things there."

Mother, her face flushed, her skin taut over her high cheekbones, turned to Lev. "Take him to the house. Let him look and see how much food we are hoarding," she said calmly, without once raising her eyes toward the soldier. He looked at her crossly but Mother turned her head away.

"Come," Lev told him. The soldier did not follow him. He turned on his heel and walked away with all the vegetables we had picked and our pitcher of milk.

The next day he was back, pushing most of our vegetables into his container. Sasha watched, an alarmed expression on his face.

"Leave some radishes for me!" he cried in his high-pitched voice. The soldier glared at him and threw a radish to the ground.

"That should be enough for you. You're only a little squirt. Pick it up, eat it. Maybe I'll even give you another." Sasha was on his feet like lightning, grabbed the soldier's hand, and bit it at the wrist with all his might. The soldier grimaced, pulled his hand away, and smacked him across the face. Sasha screamed and we were all on our feet. Sasha's nose was bleeding, and Mother picked him up and turned to the soldier.

"Aren't you proud, you vicious bully?"

Surprised, he glared at us, spat on the ground, and walked away, whistling.

"God, how I hate that man, how I hate them all!" she cried.

That night we went to bed hungry and upset. How we loathed that ungainly, tall hulk of uncivilized humanity who had the power to take our food and to humiliate us.

The next morning when Mother opened the door, we heard her gasp and ran to see what had happened. She was bent over a large wooden container covered with a thin piece of cheesecloth, her hands in midair, afraid to touch it.

"What is it? What's in the box?" we cried.

Mama turned to us. "Vegetables, I think," she said, touching the cheesecloth gingerly.

"Who could have left it?" she said softly, as if to herself.

"Do you think it's some trick?" Lev asked.

"I don't know . . ." Mother's eyes were on the box, her hands still not daring to lift the cloth.

"We'll know only when we look inside," Vitya said, starting to lift the box. Lev pushed her aside, brought it in, and placed it on the table. For a second we could only stare as Mama removed the cloth, which floated to the floor.

"Vegetables—a whole basketful!" Marina shouted as Mama's hands moved swiftly, placing carrots, onions, beans, radishes, lettuce, beets, and small, shiny, green cucumbers into separate piles on the table. We stared, wide-eyed, open-mouthed. We were mystified, almost frightened, as we watched.

"Who—who sent us all these wonderful things?" Vitya cried.

"I think we had better destroy them," Lev said adamantly. "Someone may have put poison in them!"

"No! Don't do that," Sasha cried. "I'll eat a cucumber." He grabbed one and ran to the corner of the room and started eating it hungrily before any of us could stop him. "I'm all right," he cried. "See," and he took another large bite. "I'm not dead—they are good!" he said through a mouthful of cucumber. We laughed, and Mother, still very baffled, told Vitya and Marina to store the food, and she and the girls were suddenly busy planning meals. The mood of the room changed and when the "goon," as we had started calling the soldier, came for our vegetables and milk, we paid little attention to him, something which both puzzled and, we hoped, intimidated him.

Four days later, even before we had eaten all the contents of the box, Lev found another one in the bushes near our door. This time, besides the vegetables, there was also a small chunk of pork wrapped in newspaper.

"This is a miracle!" Mother said. "When do they bring these—during the night?" She held up the greasy paper wrapping. "I suppose we shouldn't use this—pork . . ." she said regretfully.

"Oh, yes, we must!" Vitya cried. "It is meat and this is no time to think of kosher." Mother's eyes were on the meat.

"Do you suppose it is spoiled?" She touched it. "Not warm. If we cook it long enough it should be just fine." She stopped, shook her head. "Imagine pork in this house. What would Papa say?"

"He'd say 'eat it' if he knew how little food we have," Vitya cried.

"I once ate pig; this is pig, isn't it?" Vera pointed to the meat.

"You're imagining it," Mama told her, but Vera insisted that Parazka had given it to her when she went home with her one day. Mother smiled sadly. "Do you, too, wonder how Parazka is?" she asked nostalgically. We did not have to answer her. We all thought of her more often than we spoke of her.

Marina found the last basket about a week later when she opened the door early one morning to go to the outside toilet. This time the basket was heavier and packed more carefully. Instead of the thin cheesecloth for a covering, there was a brightly embroidered cloth.

"I wonder why they sent this beautiful tablecloth?" Mama fingered it. "I can't understand it."

"Perhaps they'll send us plums!" Vitya said and added, "I hope they'll give us some when they are ripe!" We smiled. Mother put the cloth on her bed and began piling vegetables on the table.

"A book!" Mother suddenly stopped; as she opened it, she cried, "And a note!" and began reading it eagerly. "Why, it's from Vasily!" she exclaimed excitedly.

"Who's Vasily?" Marina asked.

"Don't you remember Natasha Ivanovna's son, the boy who used to come to me for reading and writing lessons? His mother accused me of poisoning him when I gave him lunch one day. We sent him to Dr. Kravetsov but Natasha didn't trust him because he was a Jew, even though he saved her son's life."

We well remembered Natasha's dirty looks and how she had made Mama and Papa so unhappy.

"But why would Vasily suddenly be sending us food?" we wondered.

"Listen to this. I suppose I did teach him something," said Mother and she started to read.

Dear Madame Koshanska:

As you see, I can write, not well but you did teach me! My reading is better than my writing. I want you to hear me read, and I hope things will be good someday. Will you let me come to see you?

I am now sixteen. Tomorrow I become a soldier

of the Communist army. I am very proud to be a soldier. I hear you have trouble. Sorry, I can no longer bring food. I think of you lots. I wish I could help you. You are a nice lady.

Vasily

P.S. Mama died three months ago.

Mama touched the paper, her fingers lingering as if touching Vasily.

"Good luck; be safe, Vasily!" She spoke sadly, as if she were really talking to him. No one else said a word, and we went to bed thinking of him and of the good food he had brought us.

6

WE WERE JARRED awake by a thunderous crash repeated at short intervals. Terrified, we sat bolt upright in bed. Lev, thinking it was thunder, ran into our room to slam the windows down. Sasha and Vera started to cry and ran to Mother.

"It is not thunder," Mama cried.

"But what are those horrible crashes, these loud sounds?" Lev asked anxiously.

"Bombs, I think," Mother whispered.

"Bombs? Who's bombing us?" Marina sounded hysterical.

"It is hard to know which political faction is fighting for our town. There have been so many," Mother said. "Look out of the window!" she cried. The sky was a terrifying mass of black smoke, with drifting clouds of flame coming toward our house. "The whole town is on fire!" she said in a frightened voice. "Get dressed."

Marina helped Vera, while Vitya tried to dress Sasha.

He was still shaking, frightened and not cooperative. Mama, her eyes on the window, rubbed his back and he was soon fast asleep. Vera kept whimpering. Huddled close to the windows, we watched the fast-moving tongues of flame. The room grew so light that we were sure the fire was very close. Lev walked out and returned within minutes.

"We are in no danger from fire as yet, but with the winds . . ." Lev stopped, and we silently watched the fire and smoke, shuddering at the ear-splitting explosion of bombs now punctuated by the rhythmic firing of machine guns.

"God! What's happening?" Marina moaned.

Suddenly there was a pause so free of sound, so utterly silent, that we could hear our own breathing and the pounding of our hearts. No gun blasts, no bombs exploding in our ears, but new sounds unfolded in the distance, sounds hard to decipher. As they came closer, we recognized the screech of wheels in need of oiling, the clatter of horses, and the running, screaming, and shouting of people.

"What's happening?" Mother muttered.

"I don't know, but we must stay quiet," Lev whispered. This din, too, grew softer until it vanished. In the quiet loneliness we were stiff with fear and cold. "It is only three o'clock in the morning." Lev turned to Mother. "You and I will stay up; the rest should go back to bed."

Later, when I awoke in our sun-drenched room, everyone was up and dressed, and everything looked as it always did.

Was that horrifying fire really the result of bombs in our town or was it only a very bad dream? I dared not ask. I brushed my hair haphazardly and joined the family at the table. No one paid any attention to me.

Lev, who had just returned from town, was talking

excitedly. "You wouldn't believe it! Buildings burned to the ground, wounded people."

"What about the synagogue?" Mother interrupted him.

"I think it is all right. One of the lucky ones. Three bombs!"

"Who has our town now? Who was responsible for the bombs?" Mother asked anxiously.

"The soldiers in our house lost. Sudilkov is now in the hands of Petlura's men."

Mother gasped.

"Why are you so upset?" Lev asked. "Our town has been occupied by Bolshevik, White Russian, and other political armies, and we've survived."

"I've heard about Petlura's army," she said. "The men are undisciplined, vicious. They are not interested in law and order, but in looting homes, stores, and torturing people, especially Jews." Seeing the look on our faces, Mother tried hard to calm our fears. "We are far enough from the center of town, unless they find out that our house is big and has been used as army headquarters. Most likely we will never even see any of them," she said weakly, shaking her head.

The idea of having new soldiers in our town rather pleased me. New soldiers knew nothing about our cow; we would not have to share our milk with them, or our vegetables. All I could think of was milk, food, more to eat for us.

A sudden banging on the door startled us.

"Sit still," Lev commanded as he opened the door. Several young men in nondescript uniforms walked in. Mother's voice shook as she asked them what they wanted.

"You have nothing to fear. We are General Petlura's men; we have taken your town and we plan to keep it."

Receiving no comment from us, they looked at us suspiciously and immediately started to look under the beds. They pushed our huge trunk across the room and shook our coats and other clothing as if someone could possibly be hidden in them.

"What are you looking for?" Mother asked.

"We want to be sure you're not hiding any Bolsheviks. Better tell the truth. If we find one, we will shoot him and all of you as well."

"Look all you want. We are hiding no one," Mother said, trying to conceal her anger. They opened drawers, pounded on walls and floors. Finally, satisfied that we told the truth, they stopped. One of the men picked up an embroidered shawl resting on a chair and put it over his arm.

"You can't take this; it belongs to my daughter." Mother pointed to Marina. The soldier looked at Marina.

"She's pretty enough without the shawl, so I will take it. Maybe I'll give it back to her when I know her better." He winked at the other soldiers.

Mother turned pale; Lev moved closer to Marina.

The soldier kept looking at Marina, smiling. "We need someone to cook for us. Can she cook?" He pointed to Marina.

Mother spoke up quickly, "No, of course she can't cook. She is too young, but I will be glad to help."

Without taking his eyes off Marina, the soldier said, "Come to the house at one o'clock today. You will cook and clean for us."

Mother nodded. "One o'clock," she said softly as they walked out.

"Why in the world did you offer to cook for them?" Lev shouted furiously.

Mother looked at him sadly. "You don't understand. You just don't understand," she said bitterly. Lev questioned her no further and Mother began to plan how we were to manage our time while she was away.

"Lev, you are in charge. The children are not allowed to be outside unless you are with them. When Marina and Vitya go to milk the cow, be sure you go with them. All of you go together! You, Olya—" she stopped and looked at me—"are to help with supper."

"What about us?" Vera and Sasha cried.

Mother reached over and gave Vera a hug and picked Sasha up from his place on the floor.

"You be a good boy. Obey the others," she said.

"I will. I will!" Sasha said, returning to his boxes.

The rest of the day seemed to linger forever, with all our minds on Mama. What was she doing now? Did she know where the pots and pans were? She had never cooked before, and I wondered if by some miracle one of our old cooks had come back to clean and peel vegetables for her. Mama's hands were so beautiful when she played the piano. I couldn't imagine those hands scrubbing pots.

It had grown dark. Sasha cried for Mama in a high-pitched voice. Vera cried intermittently and complained of stomach pains. Hard as we tried, we could neither help nor soothe them. They wanted only Mother. We all wanted Mother and worried about her safety.

The dishes had been washed; Sasha and Vera had already cried themselves to sleep before Mother returned. It was pitch black outside. Mama looked exhausted. Strands of her shiny dark hair hung damp and limp about her face. We clung to her and talked all at once.

"What's the house like? Is anyone sleeping in my room?" Vitya asked.

"What about the piano? Is it closed?" Marina asked anxiously, remembering the reprimands when she left it open.

"And what about the books? We left so many," Lev asked.

"What did you cook? Did the soldiers have lots of good food and did you get some good things to eat?" I wanted to know.

Mother looked at us with a faint smile and hugged us hard. "Later. There will be plenty of time to talk about the house and the soldiers in it; but now, I have something for you."

She put her hand into the deep side pocket of her skirt and brought out four lumps of white sugar. We stared in amazement. We had neither seen nor tasted sugar for a long, long time.

"Did they give this to you?" Lev asked.

Mother lowered her eyes. "No, but they had so much sugar, I thought they ought to share some with us." She lifted her head and a tired smile crossed her face. She was pleased to have brought us something so special.

The next morning we could not keep our eyes away from the four lumps of sugar in a small blue dish in the center of the table.

"Today, we shall have sugar with our tea," Mother announced proudly. There were only four lumps. How was she going to divide them between seven of us? None of us dared ask. Mother looked as if she, too, was unsure, and we watched and waited like contestants. One lump she gave to Sasha, the next to Vera, and they clapped their hands with delight. There were just two lumps left. *How can she divide two lumps into five parts?* I was secretly praying that she would not divide, but give me a whole lump. Vera and Sasha each got a whole lump, why not me? I sat quietly watching. Mother took a sharp knife, placed it directly in the middle of the lumps of sugar and neatly broke each one into two parts. Again we waited.

"Four halves for five of us?" Marina asked questioningly.

"One half for each of you. I have had enough sugar," Mother said.

I looked at Vera and Sasha, holding on to their lumps. I hated them both even more than before! It was so unfair. They always got the biggest and the best of everything!

We drank our tea slowly, relishing the hot liquid as it passed through the sugar held at the very back of the tongue. As the tea reached the sugar, I sucked ever so gently to prolong the sweet ecstasy as long as possible. *There is nothing in the world that tastes as good as sugar,* I thought.

7

TWO DAYS AFTER Mama started working in the big house, two soldiers barged into our cottage. My mind immediately flew to the sugar Mother had brought us. Had they come to punish us for it? If they found no sugar in the house, would they still punish us? I looked at them intently. They looked friendly, even smiling, as they walked in. Their eyes moved about the room, over each of our faces, and then rested on Marina. I didn't like them before they said even a word!

"Imagine finding a prize like her in a place like this!" the heavyset red-faced soldier chuckled to the other. Marina grew smaller as she crouched behind Lev.

"Don't be afraid. We like you!" the soldier crooned softly as he moved toward her. Lev stood in front of Marina, but the other soldier grabbed him by his shoulders and threw him on the bed. Lev jumped up and pushed Marina behind him. The other soldier hit Lev in the face with his fist; but Lev, his nose and mouth bleeding, held on to

Marina. We surrounded him, crying, begging them not to hurt Lev or Marina.

"You will have to kill me first before you can hurt my family!" he cried.

"We only want this one." They laughed, their eyes on Marina. One soldier took hold of Lev, pinned his arms behind him so that he could not move while the other grabbed Marina. She screamed and kicked as he put her over his shoulder and carried her out as if she were a bundle of laundry. Lev fought to get loose, but the soldier held him in place. We heard Marina's terrified cries growing faint as she was carried into the big house. Freed at last, Lev bolted after them, but Vitya caught up with him.

"Let me go and tell Mother. I'll do it faster," she cried, dashing out, and he came back into the house. He touched his face and looked at his hand, red with blood, but made no effort to wipe it. Blood kept trickling down his chin and onto his shirt. I poured a dipper of water on a cloth, wrung it out, and held it toward him. He pushed me aside.

"Poor Marina, poor Marina," he kept mumbling. By the time he took the cloth, the blood had stopped flowing. His face was clean, but his nose and lip were swollen. I rinsed the cloth and gave it back.

"What's taking Vitya so long?" he moaned. "I should have gone myself." He paced the floor. Finally Vitya dashed in, out of breath.

"Mama knows—she's with Marina and the soldiers. She ordered me back here!" she sobbed.

Lev hit the table with his fists. "I should kill those bastards—I should." He stopped and stared.

Mama walked in, leading Marina. Both looked pitiable. Marina's blouse was torn, revealing part of her small pear-shaped breasts. Mama helped her into bed, removed her clothes under the blanket.

"Go into Lev's room," she said to us in a toneless voice and turned to Vitya. "Warm water and a towel!" Vitya acted as if she anticipated the request.

Mama began washing Marina as if she were a toy that had fallen into a bucket of polluted water. Next she got clean clothes and dressed her. Marina looked dead.

Mama sat down at the edge of her bed, suddenly shaking as if taken by a severe chill.

"Mama!" Vitya cried. "What is it? What's the matter?"

"They will soon be here—I made a bargain with them." Mama's voice was despondent.

"What kind of bargain?" Lev cried. "Those depraved disgusting beasts!"

"When they come, do nothing, say nothing. Let me handle it," she said. Lev sat down on one of the beds and put his head in his hands.

When the door suddenly opened and the same two soldiers walked in, Lev jumped up, hitting at them with his fists, but again one of them pinned his arms behind him.

"Stop being a baby!" the soldier said.

"Sit down and stay there," Mother ordered, and turned to the soldiers. "You are to keep your promise—never to come here again—you are never to put a finger on any of the children or . . ." She was interrupted by crude laughter from the soldiers.

"Or what?" one of them shouted.

"You underestimate the power of a mother when her children are hurt!" Mama said angrily. Both soldiers laughed again.

"My, my, what power you have; but let's get on with

it. Give us our reward for giving her back to you." One of them pointed at Marina. "She's a dumb ninny; there are lots of better girls in town!"

"Here's the *samovar;* it is very valuable." Mother pointed to it in the middle of the table. One of them slowly walked up to it, picked it up, knocking the teapot off the top. It fell to the floor, spilling the remainder of our cherry-leaf tea. He held the shiny brass *samovar* against his grimy tunic, very pleased with himself. The other soldier turned to Mother.

"Now the gold watch. I hope it is as nice as Gregor's gift. Get it."

Mother took the gold watch that Father had given her as a wedding present off her dress, where she always pinned it. The soldier grabbed it. Beating on the *samovar,* the first soldier walked out while the second one followed him, dangling the chain, the light dancing on the watch at the end of it. None of us said a word.

Mother returned wearily to Marina's bed. She was whimpering. Strands of her gold hair were matted to her forehead, and small rivulets of tears ran down her nose and face. She wept without making a sound. Mother held her.

"You are all right," Mother said over and over, but Marina's tears kept flowing. We watched in tormented silence. Finally, Mother stood up. She looked at us and said, "I must go back to work. They are expecting me." She waited, as if anticipating some response from us, but none of us could speak. Even Sasha pressed his face close to Vitya and said not a word.

"You all know what to do. I will be back as soon as I can."

We knew that despite her great effort, she was as frightened and desperate as we were, and was fighting hard to keep from bursting into tears as she closed the door. I looked at the others. Lev was crying; we were all crying. I so wanted to scream, to bang things, but seeing the quiet tears of the others, I buried my face in a pillow and hoped no one would hear me.

The days dragged painfully. Marina stayed in bed most of the time, crying even in her sleep. Vitya forced her to eat a little each day, but she remained pale and weak. Mother suffered the most; she sat with Marina before going to work in the big house and rushed to her the minute she returned. Marina had changed so. Her beautiful eyes had lost their luster and her lovely pink skin was lifeless and pale. Even her walk was different, and we became alarmed by the changes since the terrifying encounter with Petlura's soldiers. She clung to Mother, and in her absence, stayed close to Vitya and even to us. She was like a small child, yet she was our beautiful Marina, almost fifteen years old!

Mother never again brought us any sugar from the big house. Instead, a potato, some carrots, or a beet or two found their way into her deep skirt pockets. She also started to bring home leftovers from the rubbish bin. Potato peelings, when scrupulously scrubbed, could be turned into good soup. Carrots or other vegetables, even soft or spoiled, found their way into our pots and we marveled at both Vitya's and Mother's ingenuity in turning them into meals. Sometimes, even bones or scraps of meat were found in the rubbish bin, and on those days we had scrumptious feasts.

One night we knew something was wrong as soon as Mother opened the door. She was limping awkwardly, and the rubbish pail, which she usually carried, was not in her hand. She slumped in a chair at the table and buried her face in her hands. Frightened, we ran to her. Marina moved

Mother's hands away from her face and we gasped when we saw the bruises on her left cheek and under her eye.

"What happened?" we cried. Mother sat for a moment as if to collect her thoughts before answering us. Then she told us that two soldiers had asked her what she had in the rubbish pail, and she had told them, "Rubbish, of course." They examined it and found a half-peeled onion and a beet, which had only a few soft spots.

"These are still usable! You are stealing food from us!" they had shouted angrily.

Mother explained to them that these were in the pail because they were bruised and not good enough for their use, but the soldiers refused to believe her and insisted she was stealing. She was searched, beaten, kicked, and told that if they ever found her stealing food again, she would be shot. Mother, shaken, upset, but dry-eyed, spoke as if this terrible experience had happened not to her but to someone else. Vitya put cold compresses to her face and washed her left leg, which was bruised and bleeding.

While we were preoccupied with Mother, we heard the door slam and realized that Lev had left the house. Mother screamed, "Lev! Don't go there," and despite her injured leg, managed to jump up and dash into the darkness after him. When she returned, Lev was with her, the large butcher knife in his hand. He was shaking with anger.

"Why did you stop me?" he cried. "We let them do all these cruel things to us but not one of us dares to fight back."

Mother looked at him sadly. "There are too many of them; they have guns. They would kill you."

"So they would have killed me! It doesn't matter. I might at least have killed one or two of them for what they did to you," he shouted. The huge knife was still clenched tightly in his fist.

"You are wrong, Lev," Mother started to say, but he interrupted her.

"I want to murder those monsters! How can I live after what they did to you and Marina?" Lev slumped at the table.

Mother looked at him sadly, shaking her head. "We must stay alive and hope to be with your father again," she whispered. Lev placed the knife back into the drawer, his face full of rage.

The next day, one side of Mother's face was swollen, black-and-blue, and she walked with a limp; but at one o'clock she insisted that she had to go to work.

We soon realized the importance to us of those leftover scraps. There were now so few vegetables in our garden and no new seeds to plant. If only the cherries would ripen! We glared at the branches, heavy with shiny green-pink cherries, and cursed them for being so slow. Our stomachs were screaming for food, but experience had taught us that eating green cherries brought pain even worse than hunger.

It was quite by accident that I discovered the trees full of ripe cherries way behind the house. Searching hungrily for roots or leaves I might eat, I found the ripe cherries and was sure I was dreaming. I couldn't believe my eyes. Hunger was playing tricks on me. Plump, juicy cherries ready to be eaten! I had just seen trees full of slightly pink cherries in front of the house and stood looking at the dark luscious fruit in disbelief. Gently, I picked just one cherry, placed it in my mouth. I almost swooned. It was so sweet! I rolled it around with my tongue, slowly delighting in the firm fleshy fruit and blood-red juice. When it was gone, I held the hard smooth seed between my teeth. I wanted to savor the taste forever, but I soon lost control and started picking cherries as fast as I could and stuffing them greedily into my mouth, letting the juice dribble onto my chin, staining my blouse, but I did not care. When I had eaten so many that I was no longer hungry, I rushed around to tell the others. Within minutes we were all stained with cherry juice. Lev's face was smeared and Vera and Sasha looked like clowns, their faces were so covered with purple-red. Unable to eat any more, I dashed back to the front of the house to look at the cherries on the trees there. They were still only pink and hard, and I shook my head in disbelief.

"It is just another miracle of nature for our benefit," Mother said. Suddenly she became thoughtful. "How wonderful it would be if we had sugar. What jam we could make!" she said wistfully.

"Will picked cherries keep for a long time?" Marina asked.

Mother shook her head. "I don't know," she said, "but as soon as those pigs in the big house realize we have them, there won't be any cherries for us to worry about."

But for some reason, the men in our big house either did not care or never knew what a prize we had. But what a feast it was for us! We could stand occasional cramps far better than the pain of hunger, and we regarded our trees as benevolent providers.

8

MY MAJOR CONCERN about Vitya's preoccupation with cherries and her endeavors to transform them into meals for us was that she used an incredible amount of water. She was forever asking me to trek to the well to lug buckets of cold, clear water back for her latest culinary development. Though I sometimes grumbled, I did not mind. There was something I loved about the well—it made me feel good to attach the bucket properly, fill it, and then crank it up so I could see my own reflection in the clear, sparkling water. So this time, when Vitya requested water, I walked happily in the warm sunshine toward the well.

The sun was high overhead, casting a golden pink glimmer over the treetops. At the well, I stood enthralled, placed the pail on the large metal hook, locked it, and mechanically began to unwind the rope, slowly lowering the bucket. I was in no hurry. The splendor of the treetops held me spellbound, and it took some time before I realized that something kept the bucket from going all the way down. With my head still raised, reluctant to leave the brilliance above, I kept turning the handle to let the bucket down, but it repeatedly stopped at a certain point and would go no farther. With a sigh, I moved close to the wooden enclosure around the well to see why the bucket stopped. I lowered my head and looked down.

Staring at me with wide open eyes were the bloody, swollen faces of Dr. Kravetsov and his wife. I was paralyzed. My feet were cemented where I stood, and if I screamed, I did not hear myself; neither could I look away from those eyes staring at me. The pins holding Mrs. Kravetsov's long red hair had been loosened by the water in the well and it now floated around her like seaweed in a pool. I tried to speak—I wanted to tell them I would run for help, that they would soon be saved. Phrases kept running through my head, but I could only stand there, numb, staring. I still don't know how, but finally I turned and ran like a rabbit chased by dogs to the kitchen of the big house. Mother opened the door and put her fingers to her lips. She warned me to speak softly, not to let the soldiers know I was there. Little did she know that I could not talk! She bent down and whispered in a frightened voice, "Anything wrong? Anyone hurt?"

I said not a word, but pulled at her skirt and started to run toward the well. Poor Mother. She followed me, offering only a backward glance at the empty kitchen behind her.

When we reached the well, Mother gasped as she looked into the blood-thick water, quickly pulled out the bucket, which I had left resting sideways on their heads.

"Oh, my God! Oh, my God!" she cried, and grabbed my hand. Together we ran silently to our house. Mother told the others about the Kravetsov bodies in the well. Marina's face turned deadly white.

"How did it happen?" she whispered.

"Do you have to ask?" Lev cried. "Those depraved monsters! We take far too much from those Petlura murderers. We must take action, do something about it."

"But what can we do?" Mother's voice was helpless and hopeless.

"Set the house on fire and let them burn to death!" Vitya shouted angrily.

"There are plenty of others in town," Mama said.

"But we really must complain, show them we aren't as spineless as we seem," Lev cried.

"Shouldn't we report these crimes to the captain?" Vitya asked.

"I don't know. These people aren't human. I honestly don't know what we can do!" Mama said.

Lev was angry. "Does that mean that we do nothing?" he shouted.

"No," Mama said, "but I really am not sure where or how to do this. I feel as you do. We should not take any more brutality and must show them that defenseless as we are, we have spirit, that we would rather die than see any more of their murderous atrocities." Mama stopped and her body shook with dry sobs.

"Let's try the captain, now!" Lev cried.

"I doubt that he will do anything to make his men act less brutally—he's most likely one of them," Mama said, "but we'll go anyway."

Removing the large apron she was wearing, and turning to us, she said, "Stay in the house until Lev and I come back." She stopped at my bed. "Look after Olya," she said to no one in particular and followed Lev outside.

Marina sat with me on my bed. She kept whispering, "Sleep, Olya. Close your eyes and sleep. You will feel better."

I wanted to sleep, to erase the bloody distorted faces from my mind, but my eyes would not close. I was sure that my eyes, like those of poor Dr. Kravetsov and his wife, would remain open forever. How I wished Papa were home! He would know just what to do to get those murderers punished.

Mother and Lev were gone for a long time.

"Will Mother be limping and have a sore face again when she comes back?" Vera asked in a frightened voice. When nobody answered, her lower lip began to quiver and she said, "Nobody had better hurt Mama!"

"When is she coming back?" Sasha whimpered.

"Soon," we told him, hoping he was young enough to believe our false assurances.

When the door finally opened and Lev and Mother walked in, I rushed from my bed and hugged them to me.

"What happened? Did you get to see the captain?" Vitya asked.

"We did, and of course he denied that his men were responsible, but I told him there was no doubt in my mind that only his soldiers could have done such a dastardly deed."

"You are brave," Vitya cried. "Weren't you scared?"

"Scared? Not Mother!" added Lev. "She threatened to make a special report of these atrocities to Petlura headquarters unless they stopped." We looked at Mother in awe. . . . Her large eyes were so sad as she returned our gaze.

"Brave or not, what good have we done?" she asked as if speaking to herself.

"Of course we cannot bring the Kravetsovs back to life, but at least we let him know there was some fight in us. It was good to point an accusing finger at those savage beasts," Lev half shouted. Then he asked, "By the way, where is the main Petlura headquarters?"

Mother looked surprised. "I have no idea!" she answered with a hint of a sparkle in her eyes.

When we heard the rumble of wagon wheels, Lev rushed to the window. "They are here! Three men in a wagon!" he shouted.

"Lev, tell them to wait," Mother cried, moving about frantically, grabbing sheets from a trunk near her bed and a large white cloth from a box under her bed. She suddenly stopped and looked at our anxious faces. "You may come out, but stay close to the house, and don't go anywhere near the well. Anyone who disobeys will have to go back inside." She looked at me. "You rest, Olya. The others will soon be back with you."

I remained in the house, but as soon as they left, I got out of bed, put on my shoes, and immediately walked out the door.

Mother was busy at the back of the wagon and Lev was doing something at the well. Everyone was so preoccupied that no one noticed me. I moved close to Vera and watched with horror as they moved the heavy, waterlogged bodies from the well. There were not two, but four bodies! The Kravetsovs' two sons had been murdered also and thrown into the well beneath their parents. We learned later that Petlura's soldiers had murdered six people of the town. Five of them were Jews: our doctor and his family, and our rabbi.

The bodies were placed on sheets that Mother had spread on the wagon floor.

"Ready?" one of the soldiers asked impatiently. Mother made no reply, but quickly dashed into the house and returned with our large white tablecloth, with which she covered the bodies.

"Now drive to the synagogue; I'll direct you," she said and climbed onto the front seat next to the driver. We watched until the wagon was out of sight. Then Lev turned to us.

"Back in the house," he ordered.

We were greeted by a strong smell of burned *borscht*, which Vitya had forgotten to remove from the *petchka*. Lev locked the door, and we sat on our beds in desolate emptiness. Marina sobbed loudly, uncontrollably, and Lev's voice was harsh. "Take care of Olya! Sit with her," he demanded. Marina moved to my bed, but her sobs continued.

"Poor Olya," she whispered. "How terrible for you to have discovered the bodies."

A sudden rapping on our door made us jump, and instinctively, we huddled around Marina and Vitya.

"Who is it?" Lev asked. We waited. There was no reply. Then another loud knock. Lev reached for the large butcher knife.

"Who is it?" he called again.

"Open the door." We heard a man's voice.

"What do you want?" Lev asked.

"Don't be afraid" was the reply.

Lev slowly opened the door to a short, lean soldier whom we had never seen before.

He walked in and held out to us two large bags. No one moved to take them. We stood before him, our faces full of hatred. He was young, blond, and we wondered which of our friends he had murdered. He put the bags on the table, shrugged his shoulders, and walked out.

Lev touched the bags. "Food!" he said bitterly. "These miserable bastards! Do they think they can make us think them human by bringing us some food!" His clenched fist slammed against the table.

"Don't be too hasty," Vitya said. "Let Mother decide."

"We are so hungry!" Vera put her arm about Sasha. "Can't we even peep inside to see what's there?" she whined.

"We are all hungry," Marina told them, "but we cannot open the bags until Mother says so."

It was late afternoon when Mama returned. Her shoulders drooped, her hair was in disarray, and on her dress there were huge dried bloodstains. She sat down wearily on her bed. She looked different; she looked old.

"You must be hungry, Mama. We waited to eat with you," Marina said. Mother was lost in her thoughts. When she looked up, her voice was pierced with bitterness.

"How can I eat? I just left our doctor and his wife, their two young sons, and our beloved rabbi! They are dead. This—" she glanced at her dress—"is their blood, blood from their mutilated, swollen, murdered bodies!" She shook with sobs and continued. "Such kind, gentle people. Such senseless, brutal deaths. Please, eat without me. Let me be alone."

Vera and Sasha ran to her and kissed her hands.

"Don't cry, Mama."

Mother hugged them and sent them back to the table as she busied herself at once opening boxes and the trunk, again taking out sheets and tablecloths until she had the things she wanted. Putting them on her bed, she walked to her place at the table. In front of her were the two bags left by the soldier.

"What's in here?" Her hands were busy feeling one of the bags.

"One of the soldiers brought them here right after you left," Sasha and Vera cried.

Mother opened first one and then the other. "Food!" She sounded like Lev. "Those beasts!" She spat the words and we waited silently. "Unfortunately, we must use it, but I wish we could throw it out." She turned to Marina and Vitya. "Use whatever you need for dinner," she said.

Inwardly, we were pleased at the prospect of food but tried not to show it.

"Please have some hot tea, Mama," Lev pleaded.

Mother looked at us. "Let me change my dress," she said, and was back within seconds. She sipped her tea while Vera and Sasha ate ravenously.

"What about . . . what about . . ." I could not mention our well. Mother understood what I meant.

She told us that we would never again use the well.

"It will be filled with earth and boarded up," she said sadly. "But," she continued, "we will be getting our water from the well behind the big house."

We sat quietly, feeling wretched. As if reflecting our mood, the room darkened, and Mother asked Marina to light the lamp and put Sasha to bed. "We must all go to bed early; there is much to be done tomorrow," she said.

9

IT WAS NOT until days later that we realized the effect on us of these tragic events. We were shaken, scared, needed to be close to one another. Yet even together, we could not overcome the feeling of helplessness and fear. The sound of voices, the beat of horses' hooves, any sudden noise, no matter how distant, filled us with terror, and we waited nervously for the next disaster to fall on us. If only Father were home! What if we all were murdered? He would never know. How could he abandon us as he did? Where was he, and when would he find a way to help us? We loved him so! How could he go away without us?

Mother hated to leave us when she had to go to work for the soldiers, and when she came back she looked us over carefully as if fully expecting something terrible to have happened to us in her absence. We were all undergoing a slow change. Sasha, who used to spend hours playing by himself, now clung to us and cried a lot. The tiny creatures and pictures he produced from the small ball of clay and his crayons and paper did not hold his interest for long. He had to hold on to one of us, his large blue eyes searching our faces. Vera was always hungry, frightened, and cried during the night.

Vitya became more silent, Lev less patient and cross much of the time, but Marina changed the most. She rarely smiled and sat, withdrawn, staring silently into space. For me, it was nightmares! Nightly I dreamed about the Kravetsovs and dreaded falling asleep, cowering in bed waiting for Mother to come back from work.

One night she came into the house but did not stop at my bed, and I whispered loudly, "Hello, Mama, please sit with me." She did not reply but sat down on Lev's bed instead. I heard them talking in hushed voices. When she walked back into our room, I hoped she would come to me, but instead, she stopped at the bed where Vitya and Marina were sleeping. I felt neglected, ready to cry. Mother and my sisters whispered together in low voices, and I heard the sound of Lev's bedsprings and knew he was out of bed, dressing in the darkness of his room.

Angry and unhappy, I waited and again whispered loudly, "Aren't you coming, Mama?" When she did not answer me, I got up and walked over to Marina's bed. Mother put her arms about me. She was trembling and my fears that something was very wrong were confirmed.

"What's the matter, Mama?" I asked, feeling more frightened.

"I'm not sure—perhaps nothing, but there was so much confusion before I left."

"What do you mean by confusion?" Lev had joined us.

Mother was silent a second. "Hurried packing of boxes, things out of cupboards, and the men seemed tense," she said. "And no one checked me as I left to see whether I was stealing any of their food." We could hear the bitterness in her voice. She was silent again, and patted my hair. "Better get back to bed, Olya. If anything happens, you will know about it." Mother turned off the lamp, and I groped my way to my bed as the darkness, like swift-moving fog, filled the room. Back in bed, I did not go to sleep, but strained my ears for sounds. I heard nothing, but somehow the nothing was very loud. We heard only our own breathing and the beating of our hearts, when suddenly there was the unmistakable blast of guns at close intervals. We stayed in bed, speechless, too frightened to move. A short silence followed by more gunfire, and then strong footsteps coming straight down the path to our house. Marina began to scream and Mother ran to her.

"They are coming here, to our house," she cried. Lev's shaken voice came to us through the darkness.

"No!" he said. "Listen! They are beyond us; they have already passed." Straining our ears, we then heard the mooing of our cow and Lev shouted, "It's the cow! They are taking our cow! They can't take the cow." He started to unbolt the door. Mother's voice stopped him.

"No, Lev, no! It won't do any good." Lev groaned.

Running, shouting, and gunfire continued, and amidst all this I somehow fell asleep from sheer exhaustion and for the first time in weeks slept free of nightmares.

When I awoke, the room was full of sunshine. Lev and Mother were at the table, looking tired. Marina and Vitya, dressed, sat on their beds like statues. I quickly put on my clothes and helped Vera pull on her navy stockings. Vitya came to help Sasha dress. We did not join Mother and Lev, but sat mutely on our unmade beds. A knock on the door threw us into panic.

"Into bed, cover up," Mother ordered in a frightened whisper and went to open the door. Three disheveled, tired-looking soldiers walked in, glancing at Lev and the rest of us in our beds. We knew they were not the men from our other house. Who were they? Were they Petlura's men? They looked suspiciously around the room and at us.

"Who are you and what do you want?" Mother asked. The soldiers pointed to the piece of faded red cloth pinned to their tunics.

"We are Bolsheviks. We freed your town of Petlura's men," they announced. Mother was so relieved that she sat down very suddenly.

"We will use the big house as our headquarters, as they did," one of them said.

Mother smiled. "I hope your men will not be the brutal beasts Petlura's soldiers were."

The soldiers looked at her sternly. "We are Communists. We are here to help, not to destroy! We want to make things better for poor people like yourselves," he said, his eyes carefully examining our room crowded with beds.

"Here you are, all crowded together in the same place, when probably only a small family lived in that big house," one soldier said, pointing in the direction of our old house. Mother's face revealed nothing. He continued, "We are the first to arrive; the others of our company will come later tonight or tomorrow. We are very hungry. Have you food?" he asked. Mother smiled, looked at them. They were all so young, not much older than Lev.

"We haven't much, but we will be glad to share with you. Would you like to wash first?" Mother asked as if she were speaking to one of her own children.

Lev took them to the well, carrying a large towel Mother

had handed him. As they walked out, we hurried about making our beds, tidying things up, while Mother readied glasses and the remains of our bread. Lev soon returned with the soldiers, his black hair moist and shiny, looking so much like Father that it gave us a start.

Seated around the table, Mama turned to the soldiers. "You cannot imagine how happy we are to be rid of Petlura's murderers!" she said.

"So are we!" they shouted.

Mother served tea. "We have no sugar or real tea," she apologized.

"But we have cherry-leaf tea and it is good." Vera grinned. The soldiers grinned back at her and one of them patted her head, and putting his hand into his pocket, he brought out a shiny silver-like whistle. Smiling, he looked at Vera, then became aware of Sasha's eager face. Again, he patted Vera's head, and handed the whistle to Sasha.

"Boys like whistles more than girls," he said. "I'll find something else to give you later," he added.

Sasha could not believe his eyes. After staring at it admiringly, he put it in his mouth as if to make sure it was real, and blew with all his might. One soldier quickly grabbed him by the shoulder.

"You must not blow it now," he cried.

Sasha looked puzzled. "What's a whistle for if you can't blow it?" he asked.

"You are right, but you may not blow it now," the soldier who gave it to him said. Sasha was satisfied and kept looking at his unexpected treasure with unbelieving eyes. He hardly ate. He kept examining his whistle, and we had to caution him again not to blow it. When we finished our meager breakfast, the soldiers stood up.

"Now that the Communists have your town, things will be much better," one of them assured us. "*Spasibo*," they called as they walked out.

The days were still golden warm, and cherries still hung in clusters on the trees, yet Mother asked Lev to find the storm windows to the little house. "We must get ready for winter, windows first."

"I've never seen windows this dirty," Marina said, and Vitya brought a pail and some rags. They washed the woodwork and polished the panes. When Lev brought the storm windows, he exclaimed, "This is a lot of work. Double windows!"

"How would you like to do all the windows and storms for the big house?" Marina asked.

"We'd never finish!" Vitya said. "I wonder how Grisha did them all in one day," she added thoughtfully. We missed Grisha almost as much as Papa.

Marina and Vitya stood admiring the results of their hard work. "Clean, but so bare." Marina sighed wistfully. "I wish we had some bright bottles to put between the double windows. Perhaps this will help." She pulled the red ribbons from her plaits. "I'll tie these to a branch and lean it against the glass," she added.

Sasha watched. "This is pretty. Can I have a ribbon, too?" he cried. I gave him a green one from one of my plaits. He worked hard and got it through the round loop at the end of the whistle and proudly dangled it before us, swinging it forward and backward, and then he suddenly cried, "Put it in the window!" We stared in surprise. Surely he would change his mind, but he only put his chubby hand over it as if to give it a final hug and handed it to Mother.

"Sasha, are you sure you want to do this?" Mother asked.

"I am sure, yes," he said firmly. Lev suspended the ribbon from the lock hinge of the outer window so that the sun reflected small beams from the shiny metal. The dancing lights changed in size and shape on the opposite wall. What a difference it made and what pleasure we got from a simple whistle suspended from a green ribbon! My thoughts flew back to other times when the storm windows were put up. Parazka and Dumka cleaned colored bottles and other trinkets; Mother arranged small bunches of colored straw flowers. There were so many things to choose, and Mama often called us to see if we liked certain arrangements. What fun we had. Parazka always served us hot cocoa the day the double windows were up. How wonderful it would be to have hot cocoa now—to see Parazka!

This time, after properly praising Vitya, Marina, and Lev for their hard work, we sat down to sugarless cherry-leaf tea and thin slices of bread. Mother's efforts at cheerfulness fooled none of us. We knew how worried she was about our lack of food. The loss of our cow left us without milk, soured cream, or butter, and Vitya's soups had lost their flavor without them.

Numerous trips to town to buy food proved futile. No matter how much money Mama offered the merchants, their reply was always the same: "We have nothing for you." The merchants favored certain customers and we, as Jews, were never among them.

10

SUMMER LINGERED LIKE a doting grandmother reluctant to leave her dear ones. We were delighted and continued our lessons outside. After supper, we often sat on the grass listening to the accordion and *balalaika,* accompanied by the rhythmic stamping of the dancers.

"Russian folk music is so exciting! It is hard to sit still when hearing it," Mother exclaimed. Even Marina tapped her foot at times. It was wonderful to listen to our out-of-doors concert and watch the golden sun growing smaller and smaller until it slipped away, leaving the western sky splattered with orange-and-pink ribbons.

In spite of the chill that kept pace with the fading light, we always insisted on staying outside as long as possible. We so enjoyed the music.

"Time to come in now," Mama said one evening, and as always we begged, "Only a few minutes more!"

"Remember, only a few minutes. You must come immediately when I call." Time passed too swiftly, and when

Mama called, we regretfully started for the house only to realize that Sasha was not with us.

"Where is he?" Mother sounded scared, and Lev's assurance that he could not be far away was little comfort to her. We looked in the stable, but he was not there. He was not in his bed.

"He's playing a game; he's hiding from us." Vitya tried to sound convincing, but Mother only grew more visibly frightened.

"Where can he be?" She was really distressed.

"I'll go over to the big house," Lev said. "Maybe he's there." Lev walked briskly, without realizing that we trailed him a short distance behind.

Mother remained in our cottage, hoping Sasha would return. She was too worried about him even to notice we were also heading for the big house.

We did not dare follow Lev all the way, but stopped behind some bushes and stared wide-eyed when we saw the dancers prancing about our courtyard. Right in the middle of them was Sasha! He was dancing with such abandon and joy that Lev just stood there and let him go on until the music stopped. Startled to see Lev, Sasha tried to run past him to our cottage, but a soldier caught him in an embrace and passed him over to Lev.

"Comrade, dancing is good for the soul! You should all come and dance with us!" The soldier's voice was melodic, like his music, and in spite of his nervousness, Lev smiled and said he hoped we would be able to come back but that it was time for Sasha to come home.

As Lev took Sasha's hand and turned to leave, another soldier grabbed him just as the music started, and we saw Lev encircled by the dancing soldiers.

"You see," one of them cried, "dancing is as natural

to us Russians as breathing." Lev smiled, embarrassed but pleased.

"All right, you can take the little dancer home now." The soldiers waved toward Sasha. "But be sure to bring him back soon . . . all of you," they shouted.

Lev was startled to find us hidden behind the bushes. He gave us a disapproving look.

"You shouldn't have followed me," he sputtered, and walked so fast that we had to run to keep up with him.

When we reached our house, Mother was nowhere in sight, and the door was locked! Alarmed, Lev started banging on the door.

"Lord, I hope nothing has happened to her," he said in a frightened voice. We didn't have to wait long. Mother threw the door wide open.

"Are you all right, Mother?" Marina cried.

"Of course I'm all right!" She beamed with relief at the sight of Sasha and hugged him tight. We followed her into the house and screamed with delight when we saw Grisha seated at our table.

We rushed to embrace him. There was so much hugging and laughter that our sides ached and tears ran down our cheeks. Grisha looked thin. His hair was short; he looked older, but his face had retained the solidity and gentleness for which we loved him so. We kept hugging him and asking questions without allowing him time to answer.

"Enough questions!" Mother clapped her hands to stop a roar of disappointment. "Grisha has a very special message for us which Lev and I must discuss with him." She put her hand on Lev's shoulder. "The rest of you please sit outside and listen to the music," she said.

"Not now! We want to be with Grisha," we cried, but Mother insisted, promising to call us back within a few minutes. With our eyes on Grisha, we most reluctantly walked out.

The cheerful accordion tunes held little interest for us now. Our hearts and thoughts were in the house with Grisha.

"How wonderful to have him here," Marina said excitedly. "I hope he has news of Papa."

"I hope so." Vitya sighed.

"Maybe he brought us a lot of food!" Vera said hopefully. We laughed and tried to be patient as we waited to be called in. It was chilly, Sasha was sleepy, and we were all straining to get back to the house.

When Lev finally called us, we ran, bumping and tripping over one another to get in first, only to find Grisha gone! Mother listened to our outbursts of disappointment and anger.

"I'm more sorry than you know that you could not spend more time with Grisha," she said.

"Couldn't you have allowed us a few minutes with him?" Vitya asked angrily.

"It was too dangerous for Grisha," Mother told her.

"But we hardly saw him," we cried.

Mother smiled. "It was more urgent that we discuss something of great importance to us," she said happily. We showed little interest in her statement; we still felt the sharp sting of disappointment.

"Don't you want to know what news Grisha brought us?" she asked.

"Did he bring good things to eat?" Vera and Sasha both cried.

"No, Grisha brought us something far better than food," Mother said, holding up a letter.

"From Father!" she whispered, her sparkling eyes and flushed face revealing her joy. We immediately crowded around her chair, and she read us Father's letter aloud. It was short and had been sent to Grisha for us.

"He is safe in America!" She almost sang this phrase. "And he loves us and will send for us," she cried rapturously.

Marina, who was quiet and the least excited during Mother's reading of the letter, asked, "Will we be able to write to Papa? Why did he write to Grisha instead of to us?"

Mother's face clouded. "Our position in this town and in the country is a precarious one," she said.

"But why?" Vitya cried impatiently.

"We are not members of the working class," Mother explained.

"But Father worked. He worked hard!" Marina cried.

Mother shook her head. "He worked for the old tsarist government and we lived in a big house and had people working for us. We are considered of the bourgeois class." Mother stopped, looked at us, and said, "I know it is hard to understand. The main objective of the new government is to place material things and power into the hands of the working people."

"But we no longer have people working for us. We don't live in a big house anymore!" Vitya persisted angrily.

"The fact remains that we once did," Mother whispered sadly.

I understood little of what Mother told us and was sure that Vera and Sasha understood even less. All I cared about was whether we could write to Papa and ask him when we would join him, and blurted out loudly, "Can we write to Papa and ask when we are going to America?"

Mother looked uneasy.

"Is there still danger for us to write to Papa? Can't he write to us directly?" Vitya asked.

Mother was thoughtful for a while and there was a tremor in her voice. "Grisha has already been to the post office in Shepetovka to inquire. He was told that people in America can write to their families in Russia and that Russians can send letters to people in America."

"This must include us, too. We must be treated like all the other people in the town?" Marina's voice was sharp.

Lev put his arm around her shoulder. "We are not quite clear about this, but I will go to the post office in Shepetovka soon and get the information myself," he said.

"I will feel better when you do." Marina hugged him.

Lev returned from Shepetovka in a daze. Mother rushed to him.

"What is it, Lev? Tell us! Bad news?"

Lev shook his head as if to throw off some distressing thoughts.

"That bad?" Vitya looked at him intently.

"No, the bad news is not for or about us. Yes, we can write directly to Papa and he can write to us."

"Wonderful, wonderful!" we cried happily.

"Then why the long face, Lev?" Mother asked.

"I'm sorry. I should have told you the news first," he said half apologetically.

"What's happened?" Vitya asked. Again Lev shook his head.

"Living in a small town is like living in the wilderness. No communications, no newspaper, and we haven't seen anybody since Papa left," Lev blurted out.

"What's it to do with us?" Mother cried.

"So much has happened since Papa left."

"To us?" I asked, wondering why he was complaining now when things for us looked so bright. Lev ignored me.

"Remember, the last thing we heard from Papa was that Tsar Nicholas had given up his throne. That's all we knew."

"What has happened since?" Mother asked.

"Well, to bring us all up to date, I learned today that shortly after his abdication, the tsar joined his family in Tsarskoe Selo, the summer palace, and they, too, were all there under house arrest."

"From pictures I've seen of the place it is not too bad to stay there, even under these conditions," Marina said. Lev lowered his eyes.

"They are no longer there," he said slowly.

"Did they run away?" Vera asked excitedly.

"Hardly. They did not run away," Lev told her. "The tsar and his family have been moved from the summer palace and taken to Siberia, to Tobolsk."

There was a long silence.

"I think it is best for us not to talk about this and most of all, never to sound sympathetic to the tsarist family," Mother said. And there was no more talk about the tsar.

11

GRISHA'S VISIT AND Father's letter radically altered our lives. It was wonderful to be able to talk about Papa. He was alive, loved us, and wanted us with him in America!

Mother at once started writing him letters, always having us add a few words and sign our names. She fretted much less about firewood, and we shared her belief that the first snowfall would find us far removed from our small cottage.

Excitement increased daily as we walked to town to post our letters and to wait outside the small post office for the mail to be passed out among the people. Whenever a name was called, a joyous, happy sigh rang out from the lucky one who rushed wildly to the postman with outstretched hands.

After all the letters were distributed, those who had received nothing shared their disappointment. The postman walked back into the building, and slowly, sadly, the crowd dispersed.

"Tomorrow may be our day to get a letter," Mother would say. She always added, "Remember, America is a long way from here!" She tried not to become discouraged, but as the days turned into weeks, without word from Papa, she seemed less and less hopeful.

September was gentle, and we were grateful for the warm sunny days even though the nights were sharp and cold. The trees were almost bare, but the ground beneath felt like a soft, bright-colored carpet. We lingered with memories of diving into the leaf piles Grisha used to rake. What fun we then had playing! Now Mama reprimanded us.

"Stop playing! We must work!" We had heaps of leaves for tea and huge piles of firewood, yet Mother insisted we gather more and allowed us to use wood for cooking only, despite some very chilly days and nights.

Vitya rebelled. "Don't you think it's foolish to gather wood now? We may leave here soon!"

Mother's face looked tragically hopeless as she turned to her. "Vitya, I no longer know what to think. Father should have written by now," she said, bursting into tears.

"He'll write. It takes a long time for letters to arrive from America." Lev tried to console her, but he was not very convincing.

After walks to the post office, we returned empty-handed, with Mother more and more depressed. She seemed even more worried about our future, and we were certain that she, too, was wondering if Father had abandoned us.

Once again she started school for us, on the grass, but somehow she was far, far away even though she sat right beside us. Her mind was not on our work. Then one day a young soldier from the big house stopped and told Mother he wished he could join our lessons. His name was Igor. To her questions as to where he had gone to school, he hung his head and said, "I learned to read by myself."

Mother fetched some of our easier books from the cottage and Igor took them eagerly.

Lev said, "I wish I could go into the big house to get some of the books I have not read."

Igor looked at him. "You lived in the big house before, didn't you?" he said quietly.

Mother paled; the rest of us were uneasily silent.

"Don't worry about it," Igor said sympathetically. "I promise I won't say a word about your having lived there. But," he continued, "I will speak to the comrade Commandant this evening about the possibility of your having a look at the house."

We were delighted.

The next morning Igor came to us. "The Commandant said you may come at a time that suits us."

"Do you suppose we could come this afternoon?" Mother asked excitedly.

"That will be a very good time. The house will be empty except for a guard because everyone else will be out on maneuvers," he replied.

Promptly at four o'clock, we followed Mother up the path to our home. It felt strange standing at the door of our own house, not daring to walk in. Mother knocked several times, and after what seemed a long time, the door was opened by a very sleepy soldier. Mother apologized for waking him.

"That's all right," he said, yawning widely. "I have night duty so I sleep during the day," he explained. "Come in. You don't need me and won't mind if I go back to sleep."

"Of course not," Mother said, and he went back to the kitchen.

We stood at the open door for a moment, then started for the living room, where our family used to spend so much time. The huge room looked totally different. Our big black piano, though badly scratched, was the only recognizable item in it. Now it stood looking almost grotesque in the nakedness of the room. Marina tiptoed to it and lovingly placed her fingers on the top, but Mother quickly whispered, "Don't touch the keys. We mustn't waken the sleeping soldier."

We stood staring at the almost-empty room. Many tiles had fallen or had been removed from one wall, and dirty plaster was crumbled over what used to be our beautiful shiny parquet floors. Mother crossed the room, put her hand on the wall as if feeling for something. We watched her, mystified.

"Remember?" she whispered excitedly. "There are many hidden paneled doors." She knelt down, feeling along the floor. "Here!" she cried as she opened a floor panel. "A dry-food storage place," she said, bringing up a small canvas sack. "Dried vegetables—mushrooms!" and her hands were again below the floor bringing up several more packages. "There is one here I can hardly move. Will you bring it up, Lev?" She scrambled aside for him.

"Feels like a sack full of pebbles. Do you want it?" he asked.

"Yes, Lev, bring it up." Mama smiled and led us to the room she and Papa had shared.

Their enormous dark mahogany bed was still there, but the walls no longer displayed family pictures. Curtains were gone, as well as the chairs and dressing table. Mama made a sudden dash across the room and placed her hand on the paneling of her dressing room wall. Feeling carefully for a special place, she pushed it ever so gently and revealed a chest full of Father's and her clothes.

We could only stare; we had completely forgotten how many hidden storage cupboards there were in our house! Mother looked wistfully at the clothes for a minute; and then, with a sigh, as if hating to disturb the only remnant of her former life, she whispered, "We must take advantage of this bounty. Hold out your arms." She pulled things out and laid them across our outstretched arms, one on top of the other until the cupboard was almost empty, and then she quickly closed the door.

"Here, Sashinka!" She handed him Papa's fur hat and then led us out of the quiet house with all our treasures.

We each tenderly caressed the huge entrance door as if we were saying good-bye to a dear, cherished friend. The door of the house where each of us had been born, our home that had echoed with our laughter, play, arguments and more . . . Now, it was so empty, silent, with only one stranger asleep on the kitchen *petchka*.

12

BACK IN OUR little house, Mama, Marina, and Vitya put away the clothes, marveling at our luck in getting them, and Mama turned to the heavy sack.

"Dried fruit!" she said pensively. "I remember when Dumka was preparing it." We hoped Mother would offer the fruit to us, but she only pushed it toward the end of the table.

"Let's save this in case we have absolutely nothing else to eat!" she declared. We must have looked as crestfallen as we felt, for Mother turned and looked at us and untied the sack. The room was at once filled with the tantalizing smell of fruit. We looked hungrily at the shriveled sliced apples, pears, and plums.

"Only one each," Mother cautioned. My mouth was watering.

How wonderful to have one of each! I thought. My fingers stopped on a piece of apple, but I chose a pear. It was bigger. We lingered near the table, hoping Mother would relent and offer us another piece, but she hurriedly tied up the bag again.

Early the next morning we were all on our way to town in search of food. We were lucky. We were able to buy two large loaves of rich black bread, some barley, and a large container of lima beans.

"Today has been a lucky one for us. Perhaps our fortune will be extended to a letter from Papa!" Lev said as we joined the crowd at the post office, where we recognized many people who, like us, were also waiting anxiously. As the last letter was handed out, we turned away sadly, only to be startled to hear Mother's name called. "Anna Koshanska!"

Mother turned to us, distrusting her own ears. Was her name really called or was she dreaming?

We shouted, "Go up! Your name was called! A letter for you, Mama!"

Mother looked confused and started to run, half stumbling. We watched her anxiously as she reached the postman. No letter was handed her, and her shoulders drooped as she followed the postman into the small building. We ran to join her, but Lev held us back firmly.

"No! We must wait here," he insisted.

Within minutes, Mother came out and we gasped. She looked shrunken and walked as if she had been dealt a hard blow on the head. She had been in the post office only a few minutes, yet her eyes were as red as if she had been crying for hours. She made no effort to wipe her nose or dry her tears.

"What is it?" we asked.

Mother's voice was dry and hard as she spoke. "There won't be any letter today, tomorrow, not ever," she wailed.

"But why?" we cried.

Mother tried to control her voice. "Because all the letters we wrote Papa were never sent."

"Why not? We put stamps on them. I myself went to the post office to mail the letters," Lev said.

"Let's go home," Mama moaned and started to walk, stumbling, and Lev took her arm to steady her. We followed, exchanging glances, not daring to speak, wondering what the next catastrophe would be. We had seen Mother upset and unhappy before, but never like this. We were terrified.

In the house, Mother sat down at the table and covered her face with her hands.

"Tell us what happened," Lev demanded.

Mother made an effort to collect herself. "Our name is on a list of enemies of the new government! We can neither send nor receive mail until we are cleared by town officials," she moaned.

"Who are the officials? We should see them at once," Marina cried angrily.

"Our town officials are all one—one man—and his name is Koznikov!" she said bitterly. The silence that followed Mother's statement was frightening. Even I remembered how he had haunted Father and wanted him arrested, how he had searched for him and threatened us all.

"Is there no help? We must try everything," Lev pleaded.

"I'm to see him this afternoon at three," Mother said in a hopeless sort of way.

"Then there is hope!" Lev's voice was buoyant.

"I wish I could share your optimism. I have no hope at all," she sighed.

"He is still seething because Papa escaped, and is punishing us in every way he can," Mother continued. She was silent briefly. "I wish I knew how to plead, humble myself. If only there were some way of taking our name off the dreaded list, but I know his kind and am very much afraid of our meeting this afternoon." Mother wept. There was no way we could comfort her.

Time was endless until Marina looked at the clock and finally announced, "Time to go, Mama."

"I'm ready," Mother answered. She had not washed her tear-stained face nor combed her hair, which hung in misplaced wisps over her head.

"Are you going like this?" Marina made a face.

"It does not matter how I look," Mother replied. This was so unlike her; she always insisted on a neat appearance.

Vitya brought a basin of warm water and to her surprise, Mother sat down and allowed Vitya to wash her face while Marina combed her hair. Mother was oblivious to what they were doing to her. They straightened her dress and helped her into her coat. Then Lev took her arm.

"Come, Mama, Marina and I will go with you." Mother rose from her chair slowly and the three of them walked out.

"Bye, Mama!" Sasha called loudly, but there was no reply. Sasha looked puzzled and hurt, and ran to Vitya for consolation.

"Mother is not angry with you, Sashinka," she said, and suggested he play with his boxes while the rest of us sat, frightened and worried.

About two hours later, when we heard the sound of their footsteps returning, we raced to the door. Lev and Marina were on either side of Mother, helping her into the house. Again, we could not believe the change that had taken place in her during the short time she was gone. She was moaning and mumbling incoherently.

"Children, children, my children," she cried again and again. Vitya led Mama to her bed, where she collapsed with a cry. "My children!"

Marina undressed her and covered her with a blanket. "Are you still cold?" Marina asked. Mother did not answer her. She was on her back, staring at the ceiling and wringing her hands. Lev looked at her, shook his head, and motioned us all to follow him to his room.

"What happened? Tell us," Vitya begged.

Marina lowered her head and Lev swallowed hard.

"When we got to the post office, Koznikov did not even offer Mama a seat. He screamed at her the minute we walked into the room."

"Why was he screaming? That beast!" Vitya asked.

"He blamed Mama for Papa's escape and said that if she had been loyal to the new government, she would have reported Papa's escape and seen to it that he was caught and shot!" Lev told us.

"Father is in America; Father is gone," Vitya insisted. "He can't keep punishing us forever," she cried.

"He has every intention of doing just that," Marina spoke up.

"Can't we appeal to the head of the post office?" Vitya asked.

"We did. His name is Koznikov!"

We gasped. Koznikov was in complete control of our lives.

"What will he gain by this?" Vitya asked.

"He thinks that when Papa does not hear from us, he will risk everything and come back," Lev told her.

Vera and Sasha grew excited. "When will he be back?" Vera asked, and Sasha added, "He will have good presents for us."

Lev quietened them with a glare, and the rest of us shuddered to think what would happen if Papa did come back.

Vitya lit the lamp and busied herself in the kitchen. Marina sat on the edge of Mother's bed, stroking her hair as if she were a sick child. But Mother only stared at the ceiling as if Marina were not there. Sasha watched Mother for a long time and climbed onto her bed. He tried to snuggle up to her, but she screamed at him with such a shrill voice that he fell off in his rush to get away from her. He ran to Vitya, but she was too preoccupied to be sympathetic. He kept whimpering in a high-pitched voice.

What was going to happen to us now? Would Father really try to come back? Was there anyone who could help us? Mother . . . was she going to be Mother again when we awoke the next morning? I tossed and turned for a long time before I fell into a troubled sleep, praying for Mother to be our mother as she had always been.

13

SOME TIME DURING the night, an unbelievable cold penetrated the thickness of our blankets, and strong blasts of wind kept tearing at the door. Shivering in our beds, we huddled closer to one another. Lev dressed quickly and put Sasha under the covers with Vera and me. Ripping the covers off his own bed, he placed them over Mother, who miraculously slept. Marina and Vitya, too, braved the iciness of the house and put on layers of clothes and helped Lev build a fire in the *petchka*. It was a dark, angry night, and Marina lit the lamp, her breath curling like smoke from a chimney as she set it on the table. Sasha and Vera were soon asleep again, but I stayed awake. The wind, like some angry giant, shook the house so hard that I feared it would be blown away with all of us in it. When I finally fell asleep, I was flying through space in my bed, feeling free and weightless.

Much later when I awoke, the house was slightly warmer. I looked across at Mother in her bed and waved to her, but she gave no indication that she even saw me. Marina placed a pile of warm clothes on my bed and whispered, "Put everything on. It is bitter cold."

I climbed out of bed and stepped on the sheepskin rug, but it was so cold that I hurriedly got back and dressed under the blankets. I put on long underwear, thick stockings and a wool dress. As I got off the bed, Vitya handed me a red sweater Parazka had knitted for me. I touched it, held it to my cheek, wondering if Parazka had any idea how much we needed her.

I helped Sasha and Vera bundle up in warm clothes and we ran to the windows, but the frost was too thick for us to see through. The howling wind seemed powerful enough to push the cold through the double panes.

Vitya's call to breakfast was welcome though it felt strange to eat without Mother who was in her bed so close to the table. She was awake, again looking at the ceiling, but turned away when Lev brought her tea. There was a look of hopelessness on his face when he returned to us. I wondered if Mother had lost the ability to talk. It was frightening to have her so close, but still so distant and silent. Apparently Lev assumed that Mother could neither hear nor speak because he began to talk as though she were not there.

"We are in real trouble," he said, looking at her. "She may get better, but she may remain like this." I wanted to shout for him to stop talking like this in front of her, but when I looked at her face, my heart sank. I realized that there was a lot of truth in what he was saying.

"This miserable incident with Koznikov was a terrible shock to her," Marina said tearfully. "But I think she will get over it before long," she added.

"I hope you are right, Marina," Lev said with uncertainty. "In the meantime, we must be prepared for the worst and do things on our own if we are to survive. We must work together and take care of the younger ones."

Vitya burst into tears. "As far as I am concerned, our most important responsibility is to look after Mama and get her better," she cried.

"Of course we will look after her, but you must be realistic," Lev cautioned her. "As the oldest, I will be in charge. Things are not going to be easy for us, and I expect each of you to do your share." Poor Lev tried so hard to sound brave, but he looked like a frightened little boy.

I left the table with a heavy lump inside me that tears could not soften. What was going to happen to us? Lev was clever and almost grown, but he was barely sixteen! He was not Mother! I sat on the edge of my bed, shivering, trying not to stare at her. Vitya started to put wood into the *petchka*, but Lev screamed, "No more wood! No more wood! We must save it."

"But it is freezing," Marina said through chattering teeth.

"We have to get used to it" was Lev's reply.

Vitya and Marina looked at each other, and Sasha began to jump up and down. "It is too cold! Too cold!" he cried.

Lev paid no attention to him, and it was not until almost lunchtime that Lev finally allowed Vitya to put a little wood on the smoldering ashes in the *petchka*. We sat down to the watery soup she had cooked, listening to the angry gusting wind. The sky was a solid murky gray, making the room dark, and Marina started to light the lamp.

"No," Lev ordered. "We must save paraffin."

"I'll turn it very low," Marina said, lighting it. She did

turn the wick so low that we could see only a small circle of light on the table.

We climbed back into bed. I thought about summer days when we ran barefoot in the grass and complained of the heat. Now it seemed that the only heat I could feel was my own breath touching my hands as I blew on them. My feet felt like blocks of ice and I wondered if I would ever feel warm again.

"Please put more wood in the *petchka!*" we pleaded, but Lev refused, looking at us sadly. "This is only the beginning. We must make this wood last," he said in a husky voice.

Day after day, the storm raged, keeping us hungry and half frozen in our quaking house. The furious black clouds shrouded us in darkness and we hardly knew whether it was night or day. We stayed in bed, shivering, crying out with cold and hunger, knowing that there was no one to help us. Mother in her bed, silent, unseeing, added to our misery and terror. What was happening to us? This horrifying storm tore at our family unity, and each of us became concerned only with his own survival. Instead of sharing our bedcovers, I grabbed as much blanket as I could, knowing that Vera would be cold. No one rushed to Sasha when he cried. Only Vitya remained unchanged, human and caring. She kept feeding hot drinks to Mother and to us, and even emptied the chamber pots we were forced to use because it was impossible to get to the toilet outside. Unashamedly, blindly, we accepted her help but did not share any of the responsibility she took on herself.

One morning, after days and nights of darkness and howling icy winds, we found the sun peering through the heavy ice patterns on the windows. The effect on us was overwhelming. It was as if some spirit had touched us with a magic wand to bring us back to our normal selves. We dressed, I helped Vera put on her shoes, and Marina was taking tangles out of my hair as I was struggling to plait it. We talked to each other! We were almost human again. Marina cooked breakfast, and after feeding Mother, we sat down to our own hot tea and bread. Later, Marina and Vitya helped Lev push open the door barricaded by the heavy snowdrifts, to reveal to us a dazzling world. Except for a few delicate patterns of small animal tracks, the snow was unbroken, like pure, sparkling white sugar. The trees were coated with a sheath of shimmering ice, their branches arched downward under their heavy glittering burden. Icicles on the edge of the roof danced and twinkled in the sun like small crystal chandeliers. The cold beauty of the snow and ice touched me as deeply as did the cherry trees in bloom. Lev was bursting with energy as he shoveled a wide path. The sun was shining! Quickly we came back to being ourselves, and despite our distress over Mother, the world was beautiful.

The snow was deep with high drifts, fancifully sculptured by the wind, and Vera, Sasha, and I ran about, falling, laughing, pushing each other, and throwing snowballs. We were so bundled up in layers of clothes that only our faces were cold. It felt wonderful to move, breathe the cold air, and laugh again. The sun caressed our faces and warmed us even through our layers of clothing.

When we went in, the others were already seated at the table. Lev, in Mother's chair, was making a list of things that had to be done. "Water, food, are a must," he said.

"And help for Mama," Marina added.

"Water—easy. I can get it," I cried eagerly.

"Fine," Lev said. "We might even manage some food,

but help for Mother . . ." His voice trailed off in a hopeless sigh.

Within minutes we were in our coats, and we followed the footprints Lev made for us in the deep snow. Someone had cleared the space around the well at the big house. It looked very different amid snowdrifts and the sparkling trees. A thin layer of ice covered the water's surface and as the bucket hit it, the ice shattered, mirrorlike, into many shining splinters. I could not watch. I knew the faces of the Kravetsovs would blind me if I lingered. Lev filled two buckets and carried them easily. Vera and I struggled with a third, spilling much of it every time we lifted our feet, so that by the time we got to the house, there was little water in the bucket.

"Now, what about food?" Vitya's brow was knitted. "There is little of anything in the house. We must try again in town," she said.

Marina looked at the clock. "At this hour we wouldn't get a thing. If we go early tomorrow, we might be lucky."

Lev and Marina returned very late the following afternoon. They had nothing in their bags, and both sat down wearily without taking off their coats. No one spoke. Marina was close to tears.

"No one would sell us anything! It didn't matter how much money we offered them," she said. Vitya brought tea for her and Lev, but neither drank it.

"Drink your tea; it will warm you," Vitya urged, and again busied herself in search of something for us to eat that night. She fed Mother first and then sat down to eat with us. Sasha was still sulking and Marina tried to get him to eat his soup. Vitya was very quiet and had a strange look on her face.

"Remember when no one would sell Mother seeds?" she asked. Of course we remembered.

"Well," she cried, "we are going to get food by offering something the merchants want."

"But what do we have to use instead of money?" Marina asked, looking about the room.

"We could do without one of these sheepskin rugs we have and . . ." Vitya was quiet again. "We can offer the red woolen material at the bottom of the trunk," she added.

"We can't trade that!" Marina cried. We all knew the material, a blood-red wool that Papa had brought Mother from one of his trips and that she had always treasured. Lev lowered his head and was thoughtful for a second.

"If this will get us food, I am all for it," he said. "I don't think Mother would mind." He looked at Marina.

No one said anything, and I was suddenly stabbed by the realization that Mother might not understand and would almost certainly not answer.

Early the next morning, Vitya and Lev left for the market. The cold air rushing in as they opened the door felt good and we so wanted to go outside and play in the snow but knew better than to ask Marina to leave Mother alone in the house. We sat looking out the window, feeling sorry for ourselves, while Marina, who had heated a large pan of water, was washing Mother. I turned from the window and watched. Mother neither cooperated nor cared what Marina did to her.

I was flooded with anger. "Get out of bed and be my mother!" I wanted to scream. Instead, I grabbed my coat and ran outside the door and cried. Marina did not even glance at me when I returned. Mother was in a sitting position, leaning against Marina, who was combing her long black hair. It was badly tangled and must surely have hurt as Marina worked to get the snarls out, but Mother never winced. I looked at Marina. Her face was flushed, and she was crying silently. I felt so sad and ashamed, and rushed up to Mother and threw my arms around her, but quickly withdrew and stood back looking at her.

Holding her was like holding my doll, or wrapping my arms about a pillar on the back of the house. The woman Marina was washing was not our mother. Our sweet, warm, loving mother was no longer there! I felt as if I had fallen into deep water, unable to swim, and that Mother watched me without making an effort to save me from drowning. I climbed onto my bed and buried my head in the pillow.

Late in the afternoon we heard a crisp, crunchy sound outside and knew Lev and Vitya were coming back from market. Marina opened the door. Vitya, her arms full of packages, practically danced into the room. Her pink face shone and she looked like a winner who had just been presented with first prize.

"Don't you think I'm wonderful?" she sang, placing her packages on the table. "Look! Bread, milk, cheese, barley, potatoes, beets, and some frozen apples." She pointed to the various items and we stared in joyous amazement. "Pretty good," she said proudly. We clapped in appreciation.

"Enough food for at least a week!" Lev said happily. Vitya came back to the table.

"I also have a surprise, a very special one! Close your eyes, everybody," she ordered. I closed my eyes and all of me trembled with excitement.

How long had it been since we had a happy surprise? I hoped it was sweets. My mouth filled with saliva. New books? Toys? Warm gloves? My mind was imagining all the things this surprise might be. Vitya's rustling of paper carefully unwrapping something made me even more excited.

"Now, open your eyes," she cried, and we stared at the object in her hand. An egg! A single egg!

"This is for Mother," she announced. "Mama shall have a boiled egg today."

My eyes stung with tears of disappointment. An egg for Mother was wonderful, but I felt so let down. How I longed for a surprise, something wonderful like chocolates, new books, a new scarf. I tried to feel grateful for the egg Vitya miraculously got for Mother. But I could not stifle the feeling of painful regret that it was not something wonderful for us all.

14

AFTER A SLEEPLESS night, when Lev finally managed to prize open the door, he sank into drifts of snow almost up to his shoulders. Luckily, the howling winds had ceased, and we bundled up to help him clear a path. The snowflakes fell steadily, all in one direction, stinging our faces, quickly covering the places we had just cleared. It was a heavy, damp snow, and we were afraid the roof would cave in under the weight of it.

All day and night and all the next day, the snow continued to fall. We struggled to open our door but did not even attempt to shovel a path. Our fears reached a terrifying peak when we looked out of the window and saw nothing but snow. Indescribable panic seized us. We had some food and stayed in bed under covers to save wood, but how long could we last? Would it ever stop snowing? We began to wonder what would happen if our house became completely embedded in snow. Would anyone know? Would anyone care? This was the most terrifying thought: We were alone!

No one knew of our plight. Our mother was sick, and our only contact with the world was a partial opening of the door, facing mountains of snow.

We could not get water and it took our clouded brains time to realize that we could melt snow to make water. It was easy to fill the buckets with snow, but the cold in the house delayed its melting. It was also astonishing how little liquid a full bucket of snow yielded! It was a constant vigil to add more and more snow, then wait for it to melt. How well we remembered the previous winter when we reached for handfuls of snow to eat and how Mother used to scold us.

"Snow is not clean! Don't put it in your mouths!" But now that we were completely dependent on snow as our only source of water, we discovered that it neither tasted good nor really satisfied our thirst. Vitya and Marina kept filling buckets and pouring the melted contents into jars and pots, but it took much snow to make two quarts of water for cooking and drinking. And for some strange reason, we suddenly developed a craving thirst and were forever waiting for the snow to melt. Sasha seemed thirstier than the rest of us and was frequently out of bed, helping himself to a drink. From our beds, huddled close to each other, we often saw his pinched little face draining a jar or struggling with a half-melted bucket to get a drink. Not one of us offered him help. Warmth, love, and concern for others, even little Sasha, were frozen like the rest of our small world.

Snow and chill and an eerie darkness filled our house. The loud, mournful, moaning wind rattled against the windows and the door like some wild creature trying to get in. We listened, resignedly, when suddenly a new sound reached our consciousness. It was coming from the kitchen—moans. High-pitched moaning interrupted by hiccups.

It was Sasha! Something like a tight spring snapped in us and we jumped from our beds to find him twisting, crying, coughing, lying on the floor. Next to him lay an empty paraffin bottle. Lev bent over him and cried out when he saw us, directing his anger to Marina.

"My God! He drank paraffin! He must have thought it was water."

"There was hardly any paraffin in the bottle," Marina said weepily.

"But enough to make him very sick," Lev cried.

Marina lay next to Sasha on the icy floor trying to quiet him, but he continued to cry, his chest expanding, fighting for breath, hiccuping piteously.

"Should we put him to bed?" Vitya asked.

"I don't know if we should move him. I don't know what to do!"

"God! How can we help him?" Vitya was crying.

As we huddled around Sasha, wondering distressedly what to do, a thin shadow stumbled into our midst. Disheveled, barefoot, her hair falling about her, Mother stood there. We stared in astonishment and moved aside to let her bend over him. To our amazement, she lifted him gently and carried him to the table.

"A pillow!" she ordered, and Vitya brought one. Mother placed Sasha on his stomach with his head hanging down over the end of the table and started hitting his back with the palms of her hands. His eyes rolled, his mouth hung open, and he continued to hiccup in a frenzied way.

"Water!" Mother cried, and Vitya rushed the bucket of snow on to the *petchka* and added wood. Mother continued her rhythmic thumping on his back and finally she stuck a finger down his throat. There was a terrible rasping sound, and Sasha started to vomit over Mother's bare feet, over the tablelegs, heaves accompanied by frightening sounds, followed by hiccups. When his vomiting subsided, Mother let him rest for a minute, then ordered, "Lev, hold him up by his legs, head down!" Her fingers were once more thrust into Sasha's mouth, and again he emitted a horrible smell of vomit mixed with paraffin.

"Now put him on the table!" Mother shouted. She put the pillow under his head.

"Warm water and towels!" she ordered.

Vitya, as if expecting this request, handed them to her within seconds. We gazed at Mother. Her face was beautifully gentle, sorrowful but confident and determined. She washed Sasha's face and hands, patted him gently, and held him close to her briefly. Next, she held his mouth open and washed it inside.

"Warm water in a glass," she said without looking up, and Marina handed it to her. Leaning Sasha against her, she poured small amounts of warm water into his mouth, forcing him to swallow it. Once again she asked Lev to hold him by the legs, head down, and her fingers were again in his mouth until Sasha began throwing up the water he had swallowed. We silently watched her force Sasha to swallow more water, then Lev again held him upside down to emit it.

Sasha began to look like a well-worn puppet, bent this way and that, mouth open and closed, swung by the legs, pummeled on the belly, turned and thumped on the back. Mother kept working on him, allowing him no rest. At last, satisfied that she had done what she considered necessary, she picked him up as if he were an infant, cradled him in her arms briefly, and placed him in her own bed. He was quiet. His eyes were closed and the delicate blue veins of the lids were clearly visible, making him look almost unreal.

Gently, Mother covered him, patting the quilt carefully around his small body, wiped her feet, and sat down on the bed next to him. No one spoke. We just stood facing her. She pulled her knees up to her chin, sat rocking for a second, and finally burst into tears.

Still, we stood glued to the icy floor staring at her. Could this be the same person who'd stayed in bed for three weeks gazing steadily at the ceiling? Who'd given no response whatsoever to any of us? It was hard to believe her. How quickly she had moved! And she'd known exactly what to do to help Sasha. We marveled . . .

Mother wiped her tears with the back of her hand and as though suddenly realizing we were before her in our bare feet, cried, "To bed! All of you! One sick child is quite enough."

Silently we obeyed and climbed into our beds.

Mother, with great agility, slid off her bed, careful not to disturb Sasha, and started cleaning up. So amazed were we that we just looked on and offered no help. She then filled a large pot with snow from one of the buckets and put it on the *petchka*, adding wood as if we had more wood than we needed. Lev and Marina now offered to help, but Mother ordered, "Just stay in bed and keep warm!" They knew it would be useless to argue and obeyed.

She placed mugs of steaming hot tea on a large tray. These she handed to each of us, busied herself at the table, and returned with dried fruit and thin slivers of black bread. We felt strange and festive. Only Sasha slept, and Mother returned to her bed and sat beside him with her knees pulled up to her chin. She ate nothing at all.

"Do have tea," we begged, but Mother shook her head.

"I have been well fed by all of you these last weeks," she whispered, and sat watching us, her dark eyes bright, her long hair hanging around her like a cape, and for the first time we saw the silver strands in it.

"Do have tea!" Marina pleaded.

Mother smiled and Marina left her bed and brought her a mug of tea, which she took and raised in a toast.

"To my very wonderful children," she said quietly. We held up our mugs and stared at each other momentarily. No more was said. We were all too grateful and happy.

15

STILL THE STORM raged on. Snowdrifts and thick ice on the windows kept the house in cold dreary darkness. But Mother insisted we stay in bed under covers while she dressed, built the fire, and brought us steaming hot tea.

"Drink! It will keep you warm," she ordered. The minute Marina, Lev, or anyone else made a move to get dressed to help her, she was adamant. "You have worked too hard when . . ." She sounded sad and did not complete her thoughts. It was clear that Mother was trying to erase her recent illness from our minds. She hovered over us like a mother bird whose nest had been threatened by some vicious predator, and she was determined not to let it happen again.

Sasha's recovery was slow, and Mother sat with him, urging him to take a mouthful of this or a bite of that, but Sasha made a straight line of his mouth and refused everything she offered.

"It tastes bad," he cried, and Mother fussed and worried.

"He must have liquid or he will become dehydrated." She sighed.

"You have done everything to get him to take food. I don't know what else you can do," Marina said.

"No use dreaming about something as impossible as milk!" Vitya looked at Mother.

"As soon as the weather allows, we will go to market and get milk and other things," Lev said matter-of-factly, and we laughed. Finding milk or bread for sale was almost an impossibility, and Lev knew it.

It was hard to believe that the storm would ever be anything but ice and blowing snow again. But we were wrong. The very next morning, the room was bright, the sun fighting to come in above the high piles of snow, and we heard Sasha cry, "I am hungry! I am hungry!"

Mother, who had been working at the *petchka*, rushed to him. "Good, Sashinka! So you are hungry! We will feed you soon. Drink this now; you need liquids." Sasha hung on to the cup, drinking the tea thirstily.

"Good!" Mother cried again excitedly, and turned to us. "Up everybody," she said energetically. "We must dig ourselves out and get food. Food for Sasha, for all of us."

Mother's bright face made the room feel less cold, and we put on our warm clothes.

"I want to help, too!" Sasha called. Mother beamed, looked briefly uncertain, and told Marina to get his clothes. Dressed, he shakily walked around the room.

"It's cold!" He looked at Marina. She handed him one of Vera's old wool sweaters, which he put on over his shirt.

"I do think he looks taller," Lev said appraisingly.

Mother smiled. "He's thinner, not taller, but we shall

find food for him," she said, and quickly added, "and for us, too."

We watched him devour his as well as Mother's breakfast of bread and tea. How could we have survived without tea? Mostly hot water, but it did warm us inside!

Breakfast finished, Lev, Marina, and Vitya worked frantically to open the door and clear a path. As we followed Mother outside, we were breathless at the majestic, austere beauty before us. The bright snow was spotless as far as the eye could see. Not a mark of man or animal, and we felt as if we were the only people in the world. The branches of the dark gray trees looked like arms adorned with thick glowing bracelets of glistening ice, and the sun sparkled and danced on our faces, bidding us welcome. We gazed in silence at the splendor, relishing the cold fresh air. Lev broke the spell. "Better take Sasha back into the house," he said to Mother and, looking at the rest of us, shouted, "There's work to be done," and started shoveling energetically.

"We must make a path to get to the well," Vitya shouted, and she and Marina started pushing the heavy snow with wide planks of wood and brooms.

Luckily, again, the snow had been cleared around the well. Vitya filled the first bucket and, resting it at the well's edge, tilted it and took a long, thirsty drink. Marina and I were next to drink the sparkling cold water from the icy bucket, and Vera, who had been throwing snowballs, drank last. The water was deliciously cold, with bits of ice floating in it.

"We must hurry to take some to the others," Marina said, and we immediately felt guilty not to have taken the water to Mother first.

Mother did not rush to the fresh water the way we did.

Instead, it was Sasha who ran to the bucket, but Mother stopped him.

"Wait!" she cried. "I want to heat it a bit before you drink it." Sasha made a face, followed her to the *petchka* as if to guard the water she had in the small pot, and waited impatiently for Mother to hand him the cup. He then drank eagerly and asked for more.

"Not now, wait a little for more water. What you need is milk," she said thoughtfully, her eyes moving over his thin body.

"Where do you expect to get milk?" Marina asked. Mother smiled mysteriously.

"I'll get milk for you, Sashinka," she said. "But not today!" she added quickly. She saw our questioning looks. "I have something I think I can trade for milk," she said in a hopeful voice, patting Sasha's dark hair. She looked up, smiling. "Don't worry," she said as though reading our minds. "I will make sure there is something for us all."

Early the next morning, as Mother and Lev were getting ready to go to market, we heard footsteps outside, followed by a knocking on our door. We had not seen anyone for such a long time that we forgot all about caution or fear and quickly opened it. Before us stood Igor, the young soldier who had made our visit to our big house possible. We were so glad to see him that we greeted him as we would a dear old friend. A little surprised by our unexpected friendliness, he seemed at first suspicious, but realizing our sincerity, he beamed at us and relaxed.

"I have often thought of you," he said. "It has been a long, long time since we have seen any of you. I thought perhaps you had gone away, moved out."

"It is good to know you have not forgotten us," Mother said.

"We ourselves were away, but briefly," said Igor. "We were forced to leave by the White Armies, but we are Bolsheviks! We got the town back, and we will keep it and defend it from any other imperialist armies!"

"We are glad you are back," Mother said, smiling at him.

Igor looked at his pocketwatch. "I must rush. I am almost late to report for duty, but I came to give you some important information."

We fell silent and listened eagerly.

"Beginning today, citizens of this town are to go to the post office for ration cards."

Mother turned pale at the mention of the post office. She wavered slightly and straightened her shoulders. "Rations for what?" she asked.

"Bread," Igor said. "Each citizen is to get one pound of bread for adults and three-quarters of a pound for children every week. You must all go down to get your cards today. Anyone missing will not have a card."

Mother looked at each of us and shook her head. "Sasha has had an accident recently, and I don't think he should go out," she said.

"I would advise you to take him. Even if you have to carry him. Shortages are great and people who don't get their cards today may have to wait weeks for the next cards to be distributed." He looked at his watch. "It would be best not to tell anyone that I was here," he said, twisting his cap in both hands.

"Of course not!" Mother said and, moving closer to him, held out her hand. Igor took it and Mother, standing on tiptoe, planted a quick kiss on his cheek. He saluted in military fashion, turned on his heel, and walked out.

Dressed warmly, we started out for the post office.

The biting cold rushed at us like a frenzied demon. Walking was slow and labored. Lev, carrying Sasha on his shoulders, walked ahead, making tracks that we tried to follow. We walked, concentrating on our feet, trying to keep from falling into the snowdrifts at every turn. Mother was nervous, and we prayed that she would not have to face Koznikov again. As we neared the post office, walking became easier because the snow had been packed down by many, many feet, and we joined the long line ahead of us. As soon as we had caught our breath and were able to look around, we found that we were the only Jews in the line, and it was not long before others, too, took notice of this. A group of peasants in ragged sheepskin coats, who were far behind us, tried to push us out of line.

"*Zhide!*" someone shouted.

"They aren't supposed to get theirs until next week!" someone else cried.

"Then what in the hell are they doing here now?" came a deep male voice close to us.

Someone grabbed Lev's cap and threw it back to the end of the line. Lev dashed after it and we followed him. There was a loud roar of laughter as our places were filled by others. Undecidedly, we moved away from the line, hurt and very angry, when suddenly we heard a soft feminine voice. "Comrades, I saw what happened. Follow me."

We walked behind a short heavy lady in a long soldier's coat and hat and stopped at the very place in the line where we had originally been.

"Out! Back to your former places!" she said, and her voice was not soft.

"But these are . . ." someone spoke angrily.

"Comrades, all citizens get the same treatment—you're

no credit to our party!" She waited until they were back in their places and smiled at Mother. "Not too long now—it will be warmer inside."

We watched her walk away.

"We never even said thank you!" Marina whispered.

"It all happened so fast. Maybe we'll see her again!" said Mama.

As we neared the door, Mother paled but stood straight and even tried to smile at us reassuringly. We followed her in and found ourselves before a long table facing Koznikov. He sat between two young soldiers who filled out ration cards.

"Your name?" Koznikov barked. Mother told him.

"These your children?" he asked, counting us silently. Mother nodded. Koznikov turned to the soldier on his right. "The three younger ones don't need as much as the others; cut their rations in half," he said, writing something on paper. We were stunned—Koznikov was punishing us again!

"Our rules apply to all citizens alike. We haven't cut the rations of other small children, and we should make no exceptions here," one soldier said sternly, and for the first time we recognized him. Igor. He avoided our eyes and we moved on without a sign of acknowledgment. As we walked out with our cards, Koznikov shouted, "Don't waste any of this bread. It may be a long time before you get more!" Mother walked out holding on to the cards without saying a word.

We joined another long line at the bakery and again waited in the cold until we were finally admitted. How disappointing it was that all our rations came to only three loaves of black bread! Mother's face was serious.

"This will have to last us a whole week." Then her face brightened. "Now for the butter-and-milk shop!" she said almost cheerfully.

"Do you really expect to get butter and milk?" Marina said in a "what's-the-use-of-asking" tone.

"Yes, milk for Sasha. He needs it desperately," Mother said, and we followed her wearily into a store. It was empty except for the proprietor, who sat at a small table reading part of a newspaper page. He looked annoyed by our interruption.

"Good day, Gregor Gregorovich," Mother greeted him. He rose from his chair mechanically and faced her without returning her greeting.

"No use asking, we have nothing to sell. No milk, no butter. We have nothing!" he said firmly.

"Is your wife in?" Mother asked in a matter-of-fact manner. Mrs. Kalenkov appeared from the back of the store immediately. She and Mother moved behind the curtain and talked for a long time. The room was warm and we were glad to be out of the cold. Lev put Sasha on a stool next to the *petchka*, and we were all enjoying the warmth when Mother joined us. Her face was pink and she looked pleased.

Gregor Gregorovich Kalenkov, having returned to his piece of newspaper, looked at Mother with a perplexed expression that turned to amazement when his wife came in from the back of the store, dragging a huge sack that was too heavy for her to lift. He ran to her, talking in loud angry whispers. But his wife was determined and kept pushing the sack closer to Mother, ignoring his attempts to hold it back. Finally, he gave up and returned to his newspaper, glaring at us angrily.

"Please open it so that we can go over the items we

discussed," Mother asked. Mrs. Kalenkov looked surprised.

"Don't you trust me?" she asked in an angry tone.

Mother silently looked at her and waited, and Mrs. Kalenkov grumbled something and opened the sack. Mother bent down and took out an ample container of milk, tightly capped. We could read her thoughts—*milk for Sasha!* She bent down again and took out a package of cottage cheese, a large lump of butter, struggled to get out a small sack of potatoes, a bag of onions and two large cabbages, and a sack of carrots and beets. She held each item, weighing it in her hand, nodding her head in approval. We watched, wide-eyed.

"What about the fruit?" Mother turned to Mrs. Kalenkov. "It is missing."

Mrs. Kalenkov was angry. "You are demanding too much for the earrings!"

Mother looked worried, but only for an instant.

"Apparently you have no idea how much these are worth and don't really want them or you would not put up the slightest argument!" Mother closed her purse. "Come," she said to us, but before we had a chance to move, Mrs. Kalenkov cried, "No! No! Don't do that!" and disappeared. She returned struggling with a huge sack of dried fruit and a basket of half-frozen apples.

"These are extra," she said, pointing to the apples.

Mother's face was calm as she took out a small red velvet box from her bag and opened it. We moved closer as she held up her diamond earrings, sparkling in the dimness of the store.

"Mother!" Vitya cried, but Mother pretended not to hear her as she placed them into Mrs. Kalenkov's eager, plump hands. Carefully, Mother divided the parcels for each of us to carry home. Despite the cold and deep snow, we did not feel the icy chill nor were we tired.

What a lucky day! we thought as we walked home in silence, broken only by the crunching of our feet on the snow, our thoughts solely on the precious food we were carrying and the feast we would soon enjoy.

16

THE FOOD, CAREFULLY divided into daily portions, lasted us several weeks. Sasha grew strong and very spoiled. Vera and I resented his getting the largest share of the milk and were especially upset when Mother had to coax him to drink it. However, there was no reason for complaint. The soups and numerous other dishes Mother or my older sisters cooked were eaten by us all with great relish, except Mother.

"What's the matter, Mother? Don't you like your own cooking?" Lev asked her when he saw the small serving she gave herself. Mother, a bit ruffled by his question, smiled.

"That's enough for me. I'm not hungry."

How could she not be hungry? Not only were her portions small, but she also shared them at the table with anyone else whose plate was empty first. At breakfast I watched her carefully. Her hair was unmistakably intermingled with gray; her black eyes, larger than I had ever seen them, were sunken above her high hollow cheekbones; and her small straight nose looked longer, more pointed.

When did all these changes occur in her beautiful soft face? Why hadn't I noticed them before? Mother, feeling my intense stare, rose from her chair, and I was startled to see how thin she was. Only her stomach protruded from her skeletal frame.

I was only five when she was expecting Sasha, yet I remembered how round, soft, pink, and dimpled she was. She was so beautiful then. What was happening to her? Remembrances of Mother and Father before Sasha was born kept coming back and swam before me. We had all been so happy.

That night I fell asleep and dreamed about having a new baby in our house, but I did not want another baby! I was jealous; I hated the unborn baby because Father was so busy with Mother and had no time for me. I wanted to hurt the baby and waited for the opportunity to do so.

Mama was sitting with Papa in front of the fire, and I crawled near her chair and gave her a hard blow on the stomach with my fist. There was a sharp cry, followed by a low moan, and Father vanished.

I sat up in bed, breathing hard, painfully remembering my dream, when I heard a sound that almost stopped my heart. It was a moan from Mother's bed! I was so frightened and confused. Was I still dreaming? I was very still, waiting, hardly daring to move a muscle, and then I again heard another groan, unmistakably from Mother. I jumped out of bed and ran over to her. It was pitch black. I could not see her, but felt for her. Her cold hands took mine, and I buried my head in her chest, crying.

"I am sorry, Mama, I am so sorry I hurt you," I kept whispering as my hot tears fell on her hands and face.

Mother continued to moan softly and I began to wonder if this, too, was not yet another part of my nightmare. I returned to reality when I heard her say in a weak, tired voice, "Go back to bed, Olya. I'll be all right. The pain comes and goes." I don't know how long I stayed with her and I don't remember leaving her, but morning found me in my own bed next to Vera.

At breakfast I kept searching Mother's face. Had I really punched her? Was there displeasure or anger in her eyes? I suddenly remembered something Parazka used to say to me and I could almost hear her.

"Olya, if you don't behave, the devil is sure to get you." Was the devil in me? Had I really punched Mother in the stomach? Was there to be another child? Had I really made Father disappear when I punched Mother in the stomach? My throat felt tight. I was choking and I wanted to scream at the devil and order him to leave me, but I couldn't. I sat, not daring to look at anybody and then I heard a wailing sound. My mind moved quickly to Mother, but she was busily slicing bread and I realized that it came from my own throat. Mama was at my chair instantly, feeling my forehead.

"Olya, you aren't feeling well, are you?" she asked uneasily, leading me to my bed. She took off my shoes, pulled the covers around me, kissed me, and tiptoed away. I felt better. I had not punched Mama, but I could not fall asleep. Mama was ill—more ill than any of us realized, and there seemed to be nothing we could do to help her.

17

APRIL DAWNED SUNNY but very cold, and the ice and snow stayed thick and solid under our feet. Would there ever be anything but snow, ice, and cold, I wondered, and quickly banished the thought from my mind. Surely we would soon see signs of spring; but winter had different ideas, and like a tired old man who has found a warm spot near the *petchka*, held on with all his might and brought us more snow and cold.

Our wood was diminishing fast, and Mama and Lev began casting their eyes at each piece of furniture in the house with a single thought: "Which of these is not an absolute necessity so that it could be burned for firewood?" We huddled in bed most of the time. Lev, Marina, and Vitya took turns getting water from the well. We tried to spare Mama, but the walk to town once a week for our bread rations was essential! How we dreaded these trips. We wrapped our feet in rags and then extra socks before putting on our boots. We covered our faces with scarves, but still, we were often unbearably cold. Vera, whose boots were not big enough to allow her to wrap her feet like the rest of us, suffered the most. Mother, her head and back bent to break the full force of the icy wind, moved slowly, yet stopped every so often to make sure our faces were protected. An ear or nose exposed to the subzero Russian weather could quickly turn white, frozen. Mother was no stranger to frostbite and urged us to keep our faces covered.

"Keep stamping your feet," she said. "This will keep them from freezing," and we followed her advice whenever we could as we walked.

Waiting in the long line to get into the bakery after our difficult walk gave us the most trouble. We did not have the sheepskin coats and heavy felt boots worn by many people, and often the cold was so severe that we could barely stand it. Once inside the bakery, Mother leaned against the wall or sat down when she was lucky enough to find a chair. We loosened our clothing and wiggled our toes and removed the kerchiefs from over our caps.

Once, Vera began to cry the minute we entered the bakery. "My feet feel funny; my feet hurt!" she whimpered, but there was not a thing we could do to help her. We had to wait our turn to get our bread. When we again bundled up and left the bakery, Vera was walking strangely, kept crying, and the journey home was difficult and endless. Poor Vera! She was so miserable that even when Lev carried her on his back, she continued to sob, and by the time we got into the house, she was screaming with pain. Mother put her on the bed and carefully removed her boots and socks. Vera's toes looked as if they had been made of white dough, and Mother gasped.

"Get me some warm, not hot, water," she said, blowing on Vera's feet as she waited.

When Vitya brought the warm water, Mother dipped in a washcloth and held it to Vera's toes. Over and over she bathed them until they began to change color. The right toes turned a red-pink, but the toes of her left foot began to look like small, elongated, dark-purple plums. Mother continued warm compresses on the toes until Vera, exhausted from the pain, fell asleep.

That night Vera slept with Mother, and Sasha slept in my bed. Vera cried during the night, her small painful sounds often coinciding with Mother's.

I must help them. How? My mind raced, and I crawled out of bed and stepped on the icy floor. Before I took another step to Mother's bed, a loud whisper from Marina stopped me.

"Olya, don't go there. I've just been at Mother's bed. Vera and Mother are both asleep." I ran to her bed and she was ready, expecting me as I fell into her outstretched arms. Vitya, too, was awake, and they made room for me and I crawled in between them. Vitya was crying, quietly.

"Now we need a doctor for both Mother and Vera," I said.

"We do. If only the weather would improve, Lev will get one!" Marina replied, and kissed my cheek.

"Now, go back to your own bed." I climbed over her onto the cold floor and got into bed beside Sasha with but one thought in mind: a doctor for Mama and Vera.

About the middle of April, the weather changed at last. We awoke to a bright day. The sun, fighting to come in through our double windows, filled the room with a warm glow. We were all pleased, but I was especially grateful. Outdoors, the sun felt warm in spite of the chill in the air. I took off my scarf and lifted my face and bare head, and all of me was full of gratitude and hope.

Three sun-filled warmer days followed, and the surface of the snow piles began to look like lumps of sugar in a glass of tea, porous and soft. The next sunny day found the snow piles sinking, shrinking lower and lower, and shining ribbon-like streams escaped from the ice and danced along gaily, getting lost in the diminishing snow piles. *Maybe tomorrow the snow will all be gone!* I thought hopefully.

I watched Mother and Vera. Mother had again changed so much over the last two weeks. Her skin was tighter over her cheekbones and her nose seemed even longer. She looked so small with only a little hump in her middle, and her beautiful long hair was turning more and more gray. Vera, seated on our bed, her feet resting on a chair, looked so sad, and her usually plump rosy face was neither plump nor pink. She kept wetting her chapped lips with her tongue. My throat tightened.

"Would you like a drink?" I asked her.

"Oh, yes, Olya," she said, rubbing her left knee and I glanced at her toes. They were no longer as purple, but they still looked dark and angry. Vera looked like a sick little old lady. I wanted to cry.

To our great relief, we opened the door the next day and were overwhelmed to see that much of the snow had melted. We could actually see stubs of roots and even grass on the earth swollen with water from the melting snow and ice. We rushed through our scant breakfast and Lev got ready for his trip to Shepetovka. Mother smiled at him wanly.

"Be careful, Lev," she said.

"Don't worry, Mama." He smiled at her. "I'll be back with a doctor before you know it," he said.

We watched him walk down the road until he disappeared from sight.

18

LONG BEFORE WE SAW it, we heard the slow rumble of wheels on the sloshy road and rushed to the windows, but not seeing anything, we impatiently opened the door despite the chill. The wagon finally came in sight and stopped in front of the house. It was not an open wagon, used by most peasants to cart their farm produce, nor was it a carriage. It was a combination of both, and its occupants were protected by a roof and a door on either side. One door opened quickly and Lev jumped out. Ignoring us completely, he put his hand up to help a short, enormously heavy lady who took a long time to get her bulk out of the door. She shook herself as if to shift her massive weight into place and turned to the young man who had followed her out. He handed her a small suitcase-like black bag and Lev led them to the door.

To our silent, anxious, questioning looks, Lev smiled. "Yes, we have a doctor." The young man followed Lev and the woman into the house.

"It is good of you to come, Doctor," Marina said happily to the young man. He looked at her in surprise.

"I am Comrade Boris Rebikov; my sister is the doctor," he said, pointing to the woman, who had already removed her coat and was washing her hands. We were surprised, never having known a woman doctor before. Lev introduced us.

"Dr. Rebikov, this is Marina, this is . . ."

"I know, I know, these are your sisters and little brother," she uttered impatiently, and moved to Mother's bed.

"Mother first and your little sister next," she said, waving at Vera, who sat hunched over sadly.

"Better go into the other room," she said to us, and Lev led us into the kitchen even before she finished speaking. Crowded in the small room, we stared at Comrade Boris Rebikov, who, unlike his sister, was very thin and very talkative.

"My sister," Comrade Boris said proudly, "is a nurse who has special training to assist doctors and is therefore often addressed as Doctor. She was brought to Shepetovka from Kiev because there are not enough doctors in Shepetovka." We were crestfallen.

"But our mother is very sick. Will your sister be able to help her?" Vitya asked anxiously.

Boris laughed. "She is as good as any doctor, better than most!" he said with emphasis. We tried to relax and Lev brought Vera to the kitchen and put her on his bed.

"My sister will make you better!" Boris said. Vera smiled weakly.

"Thank you, Comrade Boris," she whispered shyly.

When his sister appeared at the door, we asked anxiously, "Will Mother be well soon?" and waited eagerly for her answer. Nurse Rebikov looked at us, as if taking time to choose her words carefully before replying.

"The only thing wrong with your mother is starvation. She has had so little food for so long that she is undernourished," she said slowly.

"Can she be made well?" we asked.

Nurse Rebikov looked serious. "Your mother is emaciated—too little food for too long." She stopped, and seeing our unhappy faces, added quickly, "With good food—milk, eggs, meat—she should get well."

"But how in the world can we get such food?" Vitya cried tearfully.

"We will get it!" Lev said solemnly, and Nurse Rebikov sadly shook her head.

"I wish you luck, my young comrade." She smiled.

"Will her stomach look different if she has more food?" I asked.

"Starved children whose stomachs extend lose them when properly fed, but as for your mother, I don't know. I think she will, too."

We laughed and watched her examine Vera's feet, and marveled that such heavy, hamlike hands could be so gentle.

"A bad case of frostbite," she said. "Luckily, only the toes of one foot!" she added, fumbling in her dark bag, bringing up a small jar. "Unfortunately, frostbite as severe as this is something you will have with you always," she said, patting Vera, "but this salve should help." She put her stubby finger into the jar and smeared green salve over Vera's toes.

"The right foot will heal completely, but the left one may give you trouble every winter. Be sure to wear loose, warm boots when you go out," she said, "and keep this and use it twice a day," she added, handing the jar to Vera.

"Is there any medicine for Mother?" Lev asked.

"I will leave some pills for the pain in her stomach. The medicine, along with the food, should make her feel better." She again fumbled in her black bag and brought out two bottles of pills and handed them to Marina. "Give her one of these in the morning, and one at night if she is in pain."

"Can I have some pills, too, or medicine for my feet?" Sasha asked eagerly. Nurse Rebikov turned to face him, tousled his hair. "Be glad you don't need any medicine," she said, and again searching in her bag produced an empty bottle. "Sorry, I have nothing else to give you—perhaps you can play with this."

"Oh, thank you!" Sasha cried, reaching for the empty bottle, looking very pleased.

While Nurse Rebikov was caring for Vera and talking to us, Mother dressed and joined us in the crowded little kitchen.

"Do you feel strong enough to be out of bed?" Nurse Rebikov asked.

Mother smiled. "Come! Vitya and Marina will make us some tea," she said. We settled around the table, and Vitya and Marina served us tea and thin slices of bread.

"You must eat at least as much as your children," Nurse Rebikov scolded Mother. "You ate only a bite of your bread and slipped most of it to a plate of one of your children. You must eat!" Mother's color deepened.

"I can't eat when I know how hungry the children are," she said softly.

Nurse Rebikov looked at her sharply. "Your children will survive, but you won't if you don't eat your share! Do you want them to be orphans?" Mother paled. "Eat when you have food before you. You can't go on starving yourself!" she said sharply, and Mother quickly changed the subject.

"Vera and I must go to town for our bread rations. May Vera put on shoes?" she asked.

"By no means, no! Neither of you should go. Shoes for Vera would be very painful, and she might get an infection," Nurse Rebikov warned. "I will write a note," she said, and reaching for the paper and pencil her brother was handing her, she wrote something quickly, signed it, and gave it to Lev. "When you go for bread rations, show this to the person in charge; you will get the bread for your mother and Vera." She looked at the watch pinned to her blouse. "Time we were on our way, Boris," she cried, starting for her coat, but turned to Mother. "I will stop to see you both in two weeks—be better!" she said.

We thanked the Rebikovs and saw them to their carriage.

As soon as they left, Lev turned to Mother. "You heard the lady doctor. You must eat. No more pushing your food to one of the younger children."

"I will, I will. I promise," Mother said, and that evening ate her soup and bread. Vera's toes felt more comfortable, and we slept a more peaceful sleep than we had in many nights.

It was a new experience going for our bread without Mama and Vera. Marina held on to the precious note to the bread-ration office, and we started out confident that there would be no problems. The ice and snow were almost gone, and the earth was full of bubbling moisture, our feet sinking into the soft mud with every step. We were in good spirits and allowed Sasha to follow his own muddy path as long as he kept out of mud that might come over the tops of his boots. He was having a good time, and we watched him with amusement.

We got in the line, slushing the mud as we moved forward. When we mounted the wooden steps leading to the office, we were told to stamp our feet and shake the mud off. Next, a peasant woman in a green soldier's cap swished our boots with an old straw broom. Sasha found this fun and was scolded by her for not standing still while his boots were being brushed. We finally got into the room and stood before Koznikov. His heavy face was clean-shaven and his thinning dark hair was neatly combed. He raised his head, his cold eyes darting over our faces.

"Name?" he snapped sharply. Marina told him and handed him the slip signed by Nurse Rebikov. He looked at it briefly. "If they are not here, they are not entitled to any bread," he said gruffly.

"But our mother and sister are sick. They could not come!" Vitya pleaded.

"And we have a note signed by Nurse Rebikov," Lev cried.

Koznikov crumpled the paper in his hand. "Move on!" he shouted angrily. "You are holding up the line."

Vitya was in tears. "Mother is sick. We need our bread more than ever."

Koznikov acted as if he never heard her, and we were soon out of line and on our way to the bakery, walking through the soft mud with unseeing eyes; mine were blurred with tears. What a difference two rations of bread made! How much less bread we had now!

Outside once more, we looked at each other, while Sasha kept exploring deeper and better mud puddles.

"Have we anything left to feed Mother tonight?" Lev asked.

Vitya and Marina were silent, trying to remember what was left at home. "We certainly don't have any of the food Nurse Rebikov wants Mother to have, but with caution, we should have enough food for about two days." Vitya stopped. "Don't you think it would be best not to tell Mother of our loss of bread?" she asked. We agreed, and walked home, our wretchedness increasing the closer we got to home.

We hugged Mother. She looked pretty as she stood preparing our lunch at the *petchka*. We kissed Vera, who was now wearing a pair of Mother's bedroom slippers over her loosely wrapped toes.

"Wash first, all of you!" Mother cried, and we were soon seated. Marina and Vitya exchanged glances.

"I think Mother used all the food we had in the house just for lunch," Marina whispered.

Vitya disregarded her remark. "Hurrah for Vera walking!" she cried. Vera smiled happily and Marina shouted, "Hurrah for Mama's getting well!"

Mother bowed, and for a brief second we all felt happy, but the cut in our bread rations weighed heavily on those of us who knew. We were so afraid Mother would ask to see the bread, to feel the weight of it in her hand; but she didn't, and we breathed more easily and sat down for lunch.

Mother took a few swallows of soup and stopped.

"You are not eating. Remember what the doctor told you," Lev said to her. She put her hand on her middle.

"I am full. I cannot eat another bite," she said.

"I can finish your bread." Sasha was reaching for it.

"And I can finish your soup," Vera cried, exchanging her empty bowl for Mother's.

"You little pigs," Vitya scolded them.

"Next time you eat Mother's food, you will be punished," Marina said angrily.

Mother raised her hand. "Don't forget, I'm here! Let me handle Vera and Sasha as long as I can," she said sharply. Marina lowered her head and was silent. Vera and Sasha continued eating Mother's food, paying no attention to our angry glares.

Luck was with us again in the days to come. Just about the time we had nothing to trade for food, we had a pleasant surprise. Igor again came to see us with the good news. In addition to our bread rations, each family would also receive a quart of milk and a herring weekly. We were overjoyed and followed his advice to get in the line very early the next morning. It was a long line, but we didn't mind waiting, and we walked home happily, clutching our bread, milk, and a pickled herring, wrapped in old newspaper.

We could not remember ever having eaten anything that tasted as good as the herring! We relished each fragment, wiped our plates with bits of bread, delighting in the tangy taste of salt, which we had so missed. It was an exciting experience tasting salt again! Even Mother ate her share and enjoyed it as much as the rest of us. The milk, which we wanted solely for Mother, had to be shared at her insistence, and Sasha and Vera received the largest share, Mother the smallest. She looked more frail daily, and her sunken chest made her stomach even more prominent. She no longer sat up straight in her chair, and often needed help to get into bed. The cries of pain which we used to hear only at night now reached our ears during the day, despite the pills Nurse Rebikov gave her. Poor Mother! She looked so apologetic when we rushed to her.

"I'll be all right," she would whisper, and we left her,

heartsick, angry at our inability to help her. Nurse Rebikov had said that Mother needed good food, but there was no food at all and Mother, like the rest of us, was very often hungry. We were utterly without hope. There was nothing left to trade for food. Sasha and Vera, their hands and faces dirty, began chewing the bark of branches. Marina and Vitya cooked soup of roots and barks, and no matter how much of it we drank, the monstrous pain in our stomachs remained.

The weekly bread allowance gave us but brief ease from this pain only on the day we brought it home. We no longer had it cut into small pieces to make it last for several days, nor did we trust Lev to cut the bread equally, but watched him cautiously, and we unashamedly licked the crumbs from the table. There is nothing that so utterly drains one of human dignity, shame, or pity as hunger!

We thought of nothing but food to still the pain, as if we were born only to eat. The way we looked no longer mattered. Unwashed, uncombed, our clothes soiled, we paid little attention to Mother's pleas for us to wash and brush our hair. When she felt strong enough, she convinced Sasha and Vera to come to her bed to have their hair combed. They stood before her, indifferent, sullen, little appreciating the effort it took.

Things grew worse. The ration of milk and herring, which was so important to us, was short-lived. After only one week, it was discontinued and we were devastated. We missed the salt in the herring and were like addicts whose drugs had been taken away. Our craving for salt combined with hunger made us wretched, and once again we became like animals.

We walked about the woods at the back of the house and barn, our heads lowered, our eyes on the ground like hungry chickens, searching for anything we might find to eat. The fresh well water, which was always so good, now swished and gurgled in our empty stomachs, and Mother was the only one who continued drinking it, but she was at times too weak to hold the glass. As I held it to her lips one day, she drank slowly, and then her head fell back on the pillow. I felt such pain as I watched her, and grabbed my sweater and ran out of the house.

19

I HAD TO get help for Mama—Parazka! She was the only
one who could help. I stopped. Would she be in trouble
because of me? Would Koznikov punish her for seeing me?
I soon dismissed these thoughts from my mind. Only Parazka could help! I would go and get her, but I would tell
no one about my plan.

It was a perfect day. The slow-drifting white clouds
under a clear blue sky all seemed to be moving in the
direction of Parazka's cottage. As I watched them, my troubled doubts of should I or shouldn't I go vanished. I knew
I was right. I had to go for Parazka! As I walked, the agonizing months since our separation, which seemed more
like years, slipped away, and once more, I was Olya of the
old days, chosen to spend the day with Parazka. Happy,
exciting, and even frightening thoughts tumbled through
my mind, and I fully expected to hear Parazka's voice.

When I got to her house, I stood before it to make
sure that it was the right place. It was, indeed! I was certain

no other house in Russia had such ornately carved, color-
fully painted window frames. The heavy door was shut,
and I could almost feel the weight of pushing it open before
I even knocked. A patch of small blue spring flowers dotted
the grass on either side of the house, and I looked at them,
remembering how much Mother liked them, and how hard
Grisha had tried to transplant them into our garden.

Timidly, I mounted the one wooden step and knocked
gently, for I well remembered Parazka's displeasure at un-
ladylike behavior. "Ladies don't bang."

I waited, sure that she was coming for I heard stirring
in the house, but the door did not open. I knocked again,
louder this time. Silence. The door stayed closed, and my
heart in me was bursting. Ignoring her admonition, I began
to bang on the door with both fists. This time I definitely
heard movement and prepared myself for a severe scolding,
but the door stayed closed. I listened carefully, and again
began to bang with all my strength, using my hands and
feet, but was rewarded with a closed door and utter silence.
Exhausted and frantic, I slumped on the step, my arms
stretched imploringly across the door. I sobbed hysterically,
banging at the door with my head and hands.

I had no idea how long I remained there. I may even
have fallen asleep squatting against the ponderous door.
When I opened my eyes, the sun was high overhead and
the back of my head and neck were burning hot. My brain
felt scrambled, and I was stiff and had difficulty getting
up. I stretched, my eyes glued to the door, still hoping that
it would open.

I did hear someone in the house—Parazka is there. I stopped.
It couldn't have been Parazka. She surely would have opened
the door! My head was whirling. The noises I heard in the
house were those of the devils in her loft! Parazka had even

said they did not like to be disturbed. I felt better, but my thoughts immediately turned. Parazka was home! I felt sick and my mouth was full of a foul bitter taste.

Undecided, I remained quietly listening, wondering what to do. I stiffly walked around the small house, looking at the colorful window frames, and suddenly bent down to pick some of the small blue flowers, but threw them down quickly. No one knew I had gone to Parazka—they would know if I brought the flowers home to Mother. I picked up my sweater, fingered it, and felt a strong stab of pain. Parazka had made it for me; she must have loved me, but here she was near me, just the other side of the door, and she wouldn't let me in. My eyes again began to sting with hot tears, and I rushed back to the step, flung my sweater at the door.

"I don't want your damn sweater. I hate you, I hate you, Parazka!" I screamed.

Joylessly, slowly, I walked home, confused, incapable of handling the bitter anger and misery in me. I had had such hope. I had failed and nothing, nothing, was ever going to be right again!

I slowed down as I reached our house and pushed back my hair and straightened my stockings, which were twisted, as was my skirt. My face felt hot, and I knew it was smudged with dust, which had settled on my wet eyes and cheeks. All was quiet, the house looked sad, deserted, and I wondered where everybody was. A new thought struck me.

How would I explain my absence? Would anyone have missed me? Quickening my step, I opened the door. The house was dark and I blinked briefly and saw that everyone was gathered around Mother's bed. No one spoke to me as I joined them.

Mother stretched her emaciated arms toward me, and I ran and put my head against her.

"Olya!" she whispered, her hands stroking my hair. The others glared at me angrily.

"You are a selfish brat," Lev said.

"We have enough to worry about without your disappearing!" Vitya said angrily, and even Marina glared at me. Only Sasha leaned against me.

"I am glad you are here and not dead," he said simply.

"Hush! Sasha!" Marina scolded him, but he paid no attention to her.

"I'm not angry with you either!" Vera put her arm around me.

When I lifted my head, Mother squeezed my hand weakly. Her eyes, sunken in her white face, were unusually bright. I kissed her cheek and walked away slowly. Vitya motioned me to come to the *petchka*, where she was stirring something in a large pot. I knew she was angry. Her mouth was tensely tight, and her eyes were half closed as she glared at me.

"You are thoughtless, selfish, and think only of yourself," she scolded.

A sharp cry from Mother brought us all back to her bed. Her eyes were open wide, glassy, her face twisted in pain. She wet her lips and moaned, "Lev! Marina! Help me!" Sasha and Vera flung themselves on her bed.

"I will help you, Mama. I will make you better. Tell me what to do," Sasha pleaded. Vera kept kissing Mother's hands, crying in a very frightened voice.

"Get off the bed. You are hurting Mother!" Lev tried to move them, but Mother motioned for them to stay. She was quiet briefly, her face relaxed.

"I'm hiding, I'm hiding, find me!" she called in an almost childlike voice. Sasha and Vera hurriedly left her and stood close to Marina, listening in amazement, frightened. Mother's expression changed, as did her voice.

"Boris! Mikhail! Where are you?" She was calling her brothers and laughed as if she were playing with them.

"I have been a good girl, *grand-mère*," she suddenly said in French, and then lapsed into German. She was thanking some official for a present he brought her, and then she began talking in Russian. Endearments for Father. Her face looked so young and happy.

"I love you, no matter!" she said. Her face clouded. She was speaking to Father's mother, haltingly, cautiously, not at all happily.

"I will be a good wife for your son, I will, I will." She stopped, shook her head as if to get our grandmother out of her mind, and doubled up, again bringing her knees to her chest, rocking with pain. Tiny beads of perspiration appeared on her forehead and lower lip. Marina wiped her face, and Mother closed her eyes and was quiet, but soon started calling Papa.

"Osip! Osip, you will miss your train. Hurry." She moved her hands as if helping him on with his coat, and suddenly dropped them and her face looked tragic.

"My children," she whispered. Her mind wandered, her face changing, and she gave another agonizing scream.

"Mes enfants sans mère." My motherless children. Her eyelids fluttered.

"She's asleep, worn out," Lev whispered, and motioned us to the table. "Father should be here!" he said angrily. "I'm the oldest, but I don't know what to do. How can I help Mama?" he asked.

"Papa is selfish. He is safe, living well. I hate him!"
Vitya cried.

Though we were alarmed and surprised at Vitya's out-
burst, no one defended Papa. We all felt that he should
have stayed with us.

Mother slept, and Lev turned to me. "Where have
you been? I knew you were up early but didn't expect you
to disappear!" he shouted at me.

"Vera and I were sure you ran away when you did not
come home for lunch," Sasha said, holding on to my hand
tightly.

I looked at him, puzzled. Was he mixed up with the
time of day? Was it already time for dinner? How long was
I at Parazka's? Would I ever be able to wipe her from my
mind? She no longer cared about us; she knew I was at her
house. I was sure she had been at home. My stomach
knotted and felt like solid granite with Parazka in it.

20

No MATTER HOW hard I tried, I couldn't get Parazka out of my mind. I was so mixed up, hating her, wishing her dead one second, trying to find excuses for her the next. Was she home? Why wouldn't she open the door? These questions kept hammering away at my brain. I could not sleep. The room, lit by the moon, was unusually light, unreal. I raised my head, resting on my elbow, and could see the outline of my sisters in their bed, and realized they, too, were awake. Mother's bed was in the shadow of branches and I could not see her clearly, but the shifting branches moved from time to time and I was able to catch an occasional glimpse of her bony outline.

I sat up very suddenly. There was an unmistakable tap at the window. I ran my hand across my eyes, looked about. No one else stirred. *Branches brushing against the window*, I thought, and stretched out on my back. Another knock, this time louder, and next a definite soft tapping on the door.

I heard Lev move in his bed; next came the sound of his bare feet on the floor and the opening of the door.

"Parazka!" he cried in a trembling voice.

Was I dreaming? It was not possible! I listened hard, feeling for my eyes. They were open. I was not asleep, and Parazka had come. I distinctly heard her voice, and as I dashed out of bed, I bumped into both Vitya and Marina on their way to the kitchen to greet Parazka. She was still in her numerous skirts.

"Parazka! Parazka!" we whispered. "We need you. Mother is very sick."

Parazka caught her breath sharply. "How about the rest of you? All well?" Her piercing eyes searched our faces through the darkness.

"Only Mother—" Lev started, but Parazka interrupted him.

"Back to your beds." She sounded as she did when we were small, and her voice produced the same effect. We obeyed. Parazka soon appeared with a small lamp, which she placed on the table, and we sat up in our beds, wondering at the reality of this.

Parazka had not changed at all. Her dark plaits about her head were black and shiny, and she wore the red ruffled skirt we knew so well. Walking up to Mother's bed, she knelt and buried her face close to Mother's.

"Parazka!" Mother whispered, and Parazka cradled her in her arms and rocked her, crooning softly, as if Mother were a small child. We watched transfixed, expecting Parazka to evaporate at any second, but Parazka proved the reality of her presence.

"Go back to sleep," she said sternly, and looked surprised when we didn't immediately put our heads on our pillows. "I will be here in the morning," she added, knowing well what was foremost in our minds. "Pay no attention. I will be moving about." She gave us one of her looks, and we slid down under the covers, but our eyes followed her.

In the dim fluttering light, Parazka bathed Mother, fed her out of a small bowl, and moved about softly between our beds, assuming we were asleep.

We did fall asleep, and awoke to the wonderful breakfast smells that used to fill the big house when we lived there. We sat up in bed, staring as Parazka bustled about setting the table, and she soon convinced us that we were not dreaming.

"Up, everybody!" she said in her voice of the big house. When we started to get dressed, she walked up to Vera and me, clicking her tongue in disapproval.

"Dreadful! Your hair is so dirty," she said, her eyes on our heads.

"Para—" I started to say. She interrupted me sharply.

"Olya, help Vera," she ordered, avoiding my eyes. I wanted to ask her why she didn't let me in, but she kept barking orders at me and gave me no opportunity.

We ate the hot *kasha* with milk that we so loved, slowly, to prolong the wonderful taste. Parazka was feeding Mother, who no longer had the strength to feed herself. She held each spoonful up to her, patiently waiting for her to open her mouth.

"One more spoonful, Anna Nikolayevna," she urged gently, and followed it with the next until Mother said, "No more, no more!"

Parazka wiped Mother's mouth and hands and straightened her pillows before she turned to us.

"A beautiful day. Too nice to stay in. Out, all of you!

Gather some wood; get some exercise." She stopped. "Vera and Olya, stay." We knew we were in for the scrubbing of our lives. She did not allow me to get water, but sent Lev and heated kettle after kettle, scrubbing us thoroughly in the round wooden tub, pouring warm water over us to make sure we were clean. Next, she combed and brushed our hair and sent us outside.

"The sun will dry your hair," she said.

The day was warm. I was delighted to find that the cherry trees were full of buds almost ready to open, and knew that we would soon again find ourselves in a pink perfumed world. Vera was picking flowers at the back of the stable, and seeing Lev at our vegetable plot, I slowly walked over. Marina and Vitya were again breaking up clumps of soil, and to my utter amazement, Lev was examining small bags of different vegetable seeds.

"Where did those come from?" I cried.

Lev straightened his shoulders, looked around, and moved closer to me. "Olya, we must tell no one. No one knows that Parazka came to us. Do you understand?" I nodded. "The government would punish her if she was found with us." He looked sharply at me. "Is that clear?"

"I won't say a word—to anyone," I said, wondering whom I might tell. We hardly ever saw anyone, even on our walk for our bread rations, or when we got in line to get into the bakery, hardly anyone ever spoke to us. Most of our friends had left our small town, many were dead. I so often felt sad and so wanted to see my friends and school-mates again, but my mind returned to Lev and the seeds.

"But how did she bring all the food and seeds?" I asked.

"We don't know. Someone must have helped her, because she stored many things in the stable," he said.

"Will she stay?" I asked with a beating heart.

"I don't know. We can only hope. It is so wonderful to have her here." He smiled. I ran up to him and hugged him in utter happiness.

With Parazka in charge, I was sure that things would go well. She would perform the miracles we all prayed for.

Within days after her arrival, we were all changed. The responsibility for us that haunted Mother and caused her so much grief and pain slowly shifted to Parazka's willing, strong shoulders. Mother looked better and seemed more comfortable. We, too, shed our guilt feelings because of our inability to help her, and were once again children, free of cares and obligations too difficult for us to handle, and we were clean! Every inch of the house was scrubbed, the bedding and mattresses had been put outside to soak up and be cleaned by the sun. The winter windows were removed and the house windows sparkled.

We were so content and happy that we failed to see that in spite of Parazka's loving care, Mama was worse. She was delirious more often and for longer periods of time, kept calling for Papa, her voice impatient and even angry at times. Parazka sat by the side of her bed, wiping her face with a cool cloth, talking to her softly.

"Rest, dear Anna Nikolayevna, you will soon be with Osip Pavlovich," or "Your brothers will be here soon." At times, these assurances calmed Mother and she would fall asleep with Parazka's hand in hers. Also, Mother cried much more often during the night. Parazka was always with her, and Lev and Marina had to beg to change places with her so that Parazka could snatch a few hours of sleep.

One warm sunny morning, Parazka opened all the windows and the house was soon full of the fresh light perfume of the cherry trees in bloom. Everything was pink and white, and my heart leaped with joy. I could hardly wait to finish eating, and I rushed outside, running among the trees, hugging them as if to thank them for the beauty and joy they brought me. I was feeling happy. Mother smiled at me as I waved before going out. I looked across the path and saw that Lev and my sisters were still working in the vegetable garden. I watched and listened to Vera's and Sasha's happy chatter as they played cat's cradle. Suddenly I had to get back into the house. Something was pulling me, and I ran the short distance, rushed in, and stood looking at Mama. Parazka had moved her bed near the open window. Her face looked pink as she tried to reach out the window to touch the fluffy pink blooms. I watched her for a second, ran outside, and started pushing them closer so that her delicate hand could reach them. Then a thought struck me. *Why not bring the blossoms to her?* I began breaking branches mercilessly as fast as I could, and with my arms full, I barely got through the door. I walked in and placed them on her bed. Mother looked up, smiled, and touched my face. I was so pleased, so proud.

I made her happy, I thought, and hastily began pushing blossoms closer to her hands and face. Satisfied, I quickly looked up. She was asleep; her face above the half-opened cherry blooms was beautifully calm, and her mouth was half smiling.

"How lovely she looks," I said softly, and walked away feeling peaceful and happy.

"Look at Mother! How beautiful she is!" I whispered to Parazka, who was at the table. She walked over to the bed, and I heard her catch her breath suddenly.

"Don't wake her," I cautioned. Parazka picked up

Mother's hand, looked at me oddly, and placed it gently on the pink blossoms.

"Olya, go and get the others," she said in a strange voice. I wondered why she wanted everybody in the house when Mother had just fallen asleep, but I knew better than to question Parazka.

21

I CALLED TO Lev and told him that Parazka wanted everyone in the house, and was surprised to see him come running, followed by the others. I wanted to shout for them
to be quiet because Mother was asleep, but they moved
too quickly for me. I lingered outside and was the last to
come into the house.

Mother was in her bed just as I had left her, with the
pink blooms around her, but Marina and Vitya were crying
and Lev's face was chalk white. Parazka, busy with Sasha
and Vera at the table, called for us to join them.

"What's wrong?" I wondered. Parazka sat in Mother's
chair and we waited.

"Now that Anna Nikolayevna—" she corrected herself—"your mother is dead—" I screamed, interrupting
her.

"She's asleep! She's asleep! She is not dead!" I ran to
the bed and lifted Mother's hand. It was cool and fell back
the way the head of our kitten did when it had died. I

grabbed at the cherry blossoms on the bed and threw them on the floor with all my might, screaming, "Mother! Mother!"

Marina could not get me to leave Mother, but Parazka firmly took me by the hand and led me back to the table. Sasha and Vera were wide-eyed, troubled.

"Will Mama talk to me and look at the picture I made for her if she is dead?" Sasha asked. He looked at our faces. No one answered him. Vera burst into tears.

"Sasha, dead people can't talk; dead people are put into a big hole in the ground." She sobbed, and the two of them ran to Mother's bed.

"Don't worry, Mama, Vera and I won't let them bury you under dirt!" Sasha cried, holding on to her hand. Parazka watched them sadly but tried to quiet them. She kept whispering as she led them to Lev's bed and then returned to us.

"I wish there was some way to let Osip Pavlovich, your father, know," she said.

"He should be here with us. He left us! Mama would not have died if he had been at home!" Marina cried. Lev put his arms about her.

"You're not fair to Papa. He would not be alive had he stayed." Marina was silent while Lev told Parazka about Koznikov not sending our letters to Papa nor allowing us the letters from him. Parazka listened, and her face twitched several times.

"It's a pity we cannot let him know." She sighed. "However, funeral arrangements must be made immediately," she said in a quivering voice. She turned to Lev. "Can you attend to this?"

Within minutes Lev was out of the house, and Parazka asked Vera, Sasha, and me to stay in Lev's room while she,

Vitya, and Marina moved about quietly. We huddled together, listening, wondering what was happening.

Lev returned with two men. Yakov, the leader, was the man who had organized the burial of the people murdered by Petlura's soldiers.

Then Parazka said softly to me, "Come, say good-bye to your mother." The others were already at Mother's bed. Parazka removed the covering from Mother's face. Lev bent down and kissed her cheek, his eyes moist. Marina and Vitya, trying to control their sobs, put their arms about her and kissed her over and over again. I walked close to the bed, half closed my eyes, and barely touched her cheek as I kissed her. Vera, her dark eyes wide and frightened, made a smacking sound without touching Mother's cheek.

"Now you go and kiss your Mama, Sasha." Parazka gave him a slight shove toward the bed.

"This is not Mama. Where is she?" he cried hysterically and ran back to Lev's bed.

Parazka made no move to bring him back. We moved aside and she bent her face close to Mother's. For the first time since we had known her, we saw tears running down her wrinkled cheeks. Murmuring, chanting, she kept her face on Mother's for a long time. When she lifted her head, Parazka looked so old! She kissed Mother's face again, pushed back Mother's hair, and pulled the sheet tightly about her head and pinned it with a large safety pin she produced from her pocket. I watched, fascinated.

The person wrapped in sheets on Mother's bed was not my mother! Mother was sleeping amid the cherry blooms. A wild piercing cry filled the room and I was screaming.

Parazka pulled me toward her, but hard as she held me, I broke loose, ran to the bed, pulled at the sheets so hard that the safety pin opened, revealing Mother's face. Marina and Parazka were on either side of me, pulling me, begging me to leave Mama, but were unable to budge me. I kept kissing Mother's cold face until Lev picked me up bodily and put me on my bed. Parazka sat down beside me.

"Olya, Mother was very sick. She suffered so!" she whispered, and as she spoke, something inside me snapped.

"It is your fault! You could have made her well; you let her die!" I cried. Parazka looked at me sadly and walked away, her head and shoulders sagging.

One of the men brought in a board, placed it on the side of Mother's bed, and her body was moved on to it. Parazka lovingly smoothed the sheets and put her arms about Mother before the straps were tightened to hold her firmly on the board.

Lev picked up one end, and the other man took the other. Led by Yakov, they walked out the door Parazka held open for them. Parazka smoothed Vitya's hair, straightened Marina's blouse, and taking Sasha and me firmly by the hand, said, "Come, time to go."

I snapped my hand away from hers quickly. She looked pained, but I did not care. Marina took Sasha's and my hands and led us out with the others.

The men walked quickly, Yakov at the head, leading the way. We followed, wondering at times where we were going and why we were rushing so until we reached the cemetery. Yakov knew exactly where the open grave was, and when we got there, Marina's hand tightened on mine and I could feel her trembling.

"Stand around the grave," Yakov said, and started to pray, mumbling and shaking to the rhythm of the soft sing-song of the prayer. Sasha suddenly walked close to the edge, looked down, and screamed.

"Don't put Mama in there! I won't let you!" he cried.

Vitya grabbed him and held him to her, his face against her dress as the straps were loosened from the board and the body was placed into the grave.

Vera uttered a strange piercing cry and clung to Marina. I watched with detachment until I realized that Parazka was not with us, and my thoughts ran rampant.

She's home with Mother, I told myself, and watched the black earth cover the body and wondered if the sheets would be stained like my hands. Yakov looked at the earth-filled grave, put the board on the top, and turned to Lev.

"You know the new government does not approve of religious grave services," he said apologetically.

"I know," Lev answered and shook his hand.

22

SLOWLY WE RETURNED to the house. As we entered, the golden brilliance of the sun shimmered over one wall, making the rest of the inside seem dark. There was a pungent smell of food cooking on the *petchka* and for a few seconds we stood inside knowing full well where we were, yet we were touched by a strangeness as if we had wandered into someone else's house. As our eyes became accustomed to the light change, we saw that the table was set and that Mother's bed had been moved to the farthest corner of the room. I dashed to it. It was empty.

"What has Parazka done with Mama?" I screamed, and began calling for Parazka. Marina reached me before Lev, put her hand over my mouth, and led me to her bed. She sat down next to me and put her arms around me.

"Olya, Olya, surely you know that Mama is dead. She is buried. You were there; you saw it," she said.

"You're wrong! Parazka was home with her. Where is she? Where is Mother? Parazka took her home!"

Lev shouted for me to stop and finally shook me very hard and put me on the bed I shared with Vera.

"You are nothing but trouble!" he shouted at me angrily. "You are old enough to know that Mother is dead, and you must stop yelling. Neither Parazka . . ." He stopped suddenly. "Parazka—where is she?" His eyes darted about the room as if expecting to find her sitting somewhere silently. He scratched his head, looked at us. "She's gone, gone, and Mother is dead!" He put his hands over his face and sobbed in such misery that I joined the others who clustered about him.

Our grief was now doubled. Mother dead, Parazka gone! It was too much to bear, and we sat dazed, hovering between reality and the possible miracle that Parazka was somewhere in the house. We stood around, silently waiting, the way one waits for a clock to strike. Vitya's voice shattered the stillness.

"There is a paper on the pillow here," she said, pointing to it on Mother's bed. We dashed to the bed, which Parazka had covered with Mother's favorite coverlet, and saw the beautifully embroidered case she had put on the pillow. Lev hurriedly reached for the paper.

"Read it to us! Read it out loud!" we kept urging. He stopped, looked at us, his eyes brimming with tears.

"Read it! Read it!" we again begged. He wiped his eyes and started to read.

" 'Sleep in peace, sleep warm, Anna Nikolayevna, child of my heart, light of my world. You left me four days short of your thirty-sixth birthday.' " He lifted the paper as if it were a precious object and was about to tuck it under the pillow, but suddenly cried, "Here's another paper!" and grasped at the folded sheet, opened it, his eyes hungrily eating the written words.

His voice was shaky as he read. " 'My dear ones: I leave you when you need me most, not because I want to. Next to Anna Nikolayevna, you are all the children of my soul.' "

"Nothing more?" we begged, hoping there was more.

"Not another word!" Lev shook his head. We sat in the darkening room.

Time stopped. The world stood still. Vitya's voice again came to us from the kitchen. "Parazka cooked dinner." She waited and continued, "I don't know where Parazka got all the food. There are so many things on the shelf." Her voice trailed back to us. We made no reply and Vitya came back from the *petchka* in the kitchen.

"Anyone hungry?" she asked in a toneless voice. Again, no one answered, and Vitya busied herself in the kitchen putting things away. She returned shortly and sat on her bed.

Sasha, whom we thought asleep, suddenly sat up and began to sob. "I want Mama, I want Mama!" Vitya held him close while Marina comforted Vera. I sat with my eyes on Mother's bed, expecting to see her, her arms move. I was so fascinated watching the bed that I hardly noticed Lev dashing around to close windows because of the sudden rain. I looked out into the darkness and heard the heavy rain beating against the window pane.

"My God! Mother will get soaked!" I dashed to the hangers where our coats and umbrellas were kept and reached for a coat, not caring whose, and dashed into the torrent, a coat over one arm, an umbrella over the other.

I ran. The rain kept pounding on my head and face. My feet beat into puddles, splashing as if trying to avoid my hurried tread as I kept moving ever faster.

By the time I reached the cemetery, I was wet to the

skin; droplets trickled down my face from my soaked hair, and I was suddenly frightened. Where was Mother? Again, as if moved by some supernatural guide, I stumbled around briefly and soon recognized the board on the top of her fresh grave. Carefully, I spread the coat over the board, sat on the edge, and held the umbrella to cover as much of the grave as I could. The density of the rain increased and beat rhythmically over the umbrella and my bare head and outstretched arms holding it. I must have been thirsty for I found myself swallowing the rain which dribbled down my throat.

A sudden loud clap of thunder followed by a brilliant flash of lightning caused me to lose my balance. I slipped, the umbrella flew out of my hands, and part of me landed on the coat, but my face landed in the mud. Mama was my main concern, and I stretched my arms out to protect her. I was surprised at the sharp sting of the rain and the frightening beauty of the sky that followed each crash of lightning and thunder. I watched the sky light up and began to count each clap: four—five—seven! That was the last crash I remember counting.

I had no idea where I was. I was enveloped in thick sleep from which I found it hard to wake up. When I finally opened my eyes, my mind was muddled, drifting like an undecided stream, and I had difficulty focusing; I could barely keep them open long enough to see the anxious faces of Marina and Vitya. I was in their bed instead of the one I shared with Vera. I closed my eyes, feeling light-headed. When I opened them again, I could, at this time, see my sisters better.

"Marina, Vitya," I stammered, but the effort to say their names tired me and once again I closed my eyes.

"Olya! Olya!" Marina's voice came to me from a distance, yet I could feel her holding my hand. I was so tired, too tired to look at them again.

When I next awoke, the lamp was lit and Lev's face swam before me. "You are all right, Olya," he said.

Vitya brought tea to the bed, and I found it difficult to open my mouth but sipped the hot liquid slowly. Marina bent her head close to my face.

"Olya, dear Olya, we have been so worried about you, but thank God, you are better," she whispered.

Better than what? What was the matter? It took too much effort to think and I dozed until morning, when I woke to find Sasha and Vera peeping at me. I tried to smile. Sasha grinned widely.

"This is for you!" he said, holding something in both hands. I made no move to take it and he looked disappointed. I weakly raised my hand and he placed his precious whistle in it. "This is for you because you didn't die and we didn't have to bury you," he said.

"Stop talking so much!" Marina scolded him, and he seemed relieved to leave my bed. Marina sat down on the edge of my bed.

"What happened? Why am I in your bed?" I asked, perplexed.

"You were very, very sick, Olya," she said, softly caressing my hand. I closed my eyes and Marina tiptoed away, but I was by no means asleep. My mind was a whirl. I was trying to remember. When did I get sick? What had happened to me? My whole being quivered with unanswered questions.

I fell again into a heavy sleep from which it seemed impossible to wake. Something heavy was over me. I was covered with a thick crust of sticky mud, making it hard for me to move, and I had difficulty breathing. My anguished cries brought everyone to my bed.

"She's worse again!" Vitya cried, and shook me gently. To my great relief, I was clean; there was no mud over me! I sipped the liquid someone fed me and slept again with utter unawareness of time.

I awoke again to a thick stillness enmeshed in pitch blackness and was suddenly full of terror. My skin felt strange. I could barely move! My hand slowly reached my face. I was not covered with mud! Relieved, I stretched, adjusting my eyes to the room. It was night, and it took me some time to distinguish between the pitch blackness lurking in some spots, while other parts of the room were aglow with a silvery ghost-like sparkle of the bright moon. My eyes traveled from the dark corners to the shimmering light, looking at things, until they found Mother's bed. I raised myself slightly. It was very dark and I was concentrating hard, wondering what I would see in the bed. "Mama?"

My head began to whirl and I sank back on my pillow. Everything was clear now. Mother was dead! I covered my face to stifle a cry, and when I touched my head, all dams within me burst, and I began to scream, clutching at the few strands of hair on my head!

"Where's my hair?"

Lev and Marina, followed by the others, rushed to my bed. "Where is my hair?" I screamed again.

Marina lit the lamp and brought it close to my bed. "Olya, your illness made your hair fall out," she said.

"It will grow back in time." Lev tried to comfort me, but I would not be comforted.

I remained in bed sleeping, crying, crying, and sleeping. My sisters and brothers accepted my condition, and

Vitya or Marina never failed to bring me some watery soup or tea and bread. There was less concern and certainly no sympathy as days dragged into weeks.

One morning early when I asked Marina for the chamber pot, she looked at me. "Olya, aren't you now strong enough to use the toilet outside?"

I was both surprised and ashamed. "From now on I will dress and not bother you," I whispered, but the minute I spoke I was sorry, because I was scared. I did not want the others to see me. Though I had not looked in the mirror, I could well imagine what I looked like.

"Bald! How awful!" I shuddered, wishing that I could close my eyes and return to oblivion, die.

23

THE NEXT MORNING, however, I kept my promise to Marina. I put on the clothes she brought me, but when I looked in the mirror, I quickly climbed back into bed.

"I can't go out like this," I sobbed, feeling my head.

"It will grow back, Olya," Marina coaxed. "Here, wear this." She tossed me a bright-colored kerchief. I put it on, and without daring to look in the mirror again, walked outside. I felt shaky, weak, and very confused. What happened to time? My last remembrance of the outside was a world of cherry trees in bloom, the pungent smell of earth-growing things, the vibrant colors of wild flowers, and—my mother's death.

Where had I been since then? Part of me, a corner of my small world, had been completely shut out, and part of me had vanished with it. How much time had passed?

The cherry trees now looked sad, and I stood in the middle of the orchard, bewildered. I had missed the miraculous change from bloom to the small shiny green and then dark blood-red cherries. Now the leaves, no longer proud and shiny, looked as if they knew their work was done, and were sadly waiting for their last long sleep.

Adjusting the kerchief on my head, I sat down on the soft carpet of leaves, pulling at all I could recall of last year, when I first discovered the ripe cherries. Suddenly water loomed big in my mind, and I almost felt the weight of the buckets of water Vitya demanded me to bring her to prepare and cook cherries.

What did Vitya do with the cherries this summer? Who got the water for her? I got to my feet and slowly walked to the well, remembering the trodden path. I stared at our big house through the spaces between heavy branches. It was silent, no one was out, and I felt a strong urge to walk close to it, to touch it, but my eye was suddenly arrested by a brilliant spot of yellow in the distance, and I hastened my step and came to a huge sunflower plant. It was dry and almost ripe. I looked in wonder at the size and beauty of it, and remembered how I used to love the plump seeds. I spotted Vitya in the vegetable garden. I could not believe it! The last time I was there, potatoes and other vegetables were not even planted!

"Olya! Olya!" Vitya called. I moved toward her slowly. "Feeling better?" she asked, looking at me intently.

"Yes, but I am so mixed up," I said.

"You have been very sick. Now you are better, and you look good!" She smiled. Self-consciously, I drew the kerchief tighter about my head.

"Why?" she asked, pointing to my kerchief. I hung my head, tears welling up in my eyes. She quickly dropped her spade, rushed and put her arms about me. But after a moment, she gently pushed me back so she could see me clearly. "It may be hard for you to see it, but your hair is really growing back," she said excitedly.

"How do you know?" I asked, not appreciating her encouragement. "I touched it this morning and there are only a few soft wisps," I said wretchedly.

"You should have felt your head when your hair first fell out. Most of it was as smooth as your face!"

I quickly moved the kerchief down my neck, and the fingers of both my hands meticulously searched every spot of my head. Yes, it was true! There were fuzzy spots of soft hair. I threw my head-covering to the ground and began to laugh joyously. Vitya again put her arms about me, and we both laughed and hugged each other, rocking back and forth until we were out of breath. We sat down on the ground very suddenly and looked at each other silently, not as sisters but as friends who had been very close and who had not seen each other in a long, long time.

"Olya, so much happened while you were sick. . . ." She looked around. "And much more is going to happen," she said mysteriously.

"What changes? What is going to happen? You are so happy! Why?" I asked.

Vitya's expression changed. Her smile faded and she picked up her spade. "I must look to see if there are any potatoes left," she said hurriedly, avoiding my eyes.

What blundering stupid thing have I done now to bring about such a sudden change in Vitya? I wondered, feeling very mixed up.

Vitya handed me a bag. "Hold this," she said, and started putting potatoes in it. "Nine!" She beamed at me. "Better than I expected. We will have potato soup."

I was not listening to her. I was carefully repeating in

my mind the things Vitya and I had said to each other. What had I done to bring about such a change in her?

"Aren't you pleased we are to have good potato soup?" she persisted.

I nodded absentmindedly and we walked back to the house.

Marina and Lev were so absorbed in their conversation that they did not hear us come in. When they did, Marina called, "Olya, come and sit with us," and I was glad to sit down at the table next to her. She and Lev looked at me for a long time.

"Olya, we are so glad you are better." I wondered why Lev sounded so sad in telling me this.

Marina pressed my fingers in her hand. "We have something very important to tell you," she said, looking at Lev, and a feeling of uneasiness came over me.

"What?" I asked.

"You see, you have been sick for so long," Lev started and stopped. "We did not think you were going to—to live," he added with some difficulty.

I was silent, completely bewildered. "I am well now!" I slid off the chair. "See, I am well; even my hair is growing again." I tried to sound more optimistic than I felt. They were silent and I looked at their serious faces.

"You try it, Marina." Lev spoke to her as if I were not there.

Marina took both my hands in hers, and her voice trembled. "You see, Olya, we will be leaving Russia very soon."

My mind suddenly cleared. I was well, strong, and cried, "Wonderful, Marina!" and threw my arms about her. She opened her mouth to speak, but I interrupted her.

"How did it happen? When? Koznikov—no more trouble? When did Papa's letter come?" The questions kept pouring out of me without my waiting for answers.

"Slow down, Olya!" Lev scolded, pulling me back to my chair. "Listen! Shortly after we found you—" his voice became husky— "Grisha came here."

"Go on, go on!" I begged, sorry for having missed Grisha.

"He helped us revive you. You were almost . . ." He stopped. "Dead. You were very sick. Grisha brought food and helped us. Then, for many weeks we heard nothing from him. We were afraid he was in trouble because of us, but he returned. This time he brought us a letter and papers."

"A letter from Papa! Can I see it? Where is it?" I cried.

"It was not from Papa, but from some American Jewish organization called the HIAS."

My face fell.

"Papa had been informed of Mama's death by Grisha, and Papa asked for help to get us to America."

All this was more wonderful than I hoped for. Papa knew and still wanted us. My excitement mounted. "When do we go?" I asked excitedly.

Lev stopped. "You don't understand; let me finish!" he scolded, as I tried to calm my beating heart and the excitement in me.

"I had to fill out papers for each of us, name, age, birthday."

"Go on!" I disobeyed impatiently. Why all the details?

Lev stopped, looked at me. "I'm trying to tell you something and you keep interrupting!" He sounded cross. I composed my face, which I turned to him, ready to listen.

"You see, Olya," he continued, "when the papers came, you were so very sick that not even Grisha thought you would recover."

I waited and was baffled by his unhappy face and the way he kept cracking his knuckles and biting his lip.

Marina gave him a sympathetic look, and turned to me. "You are not coming with us. You will stay with Nurse Rebikov and her family," she said hastily.

I stared at both of them in horror. "You can't leave me!" I sobbed. "You cannot make me stay here! Wherever you go, I go with you!" I cried.

"But arrangements have been made for only five of us. Your name is not listed."

"I don't care! I leave when you do!" I screamed so shrilly that my ears began to ring.

"Olya, don't be crazy, sshh! This is hard on us, too, but Nurse Rebikov likes you. Remember her?" He looked at me angrily. "Being sick has made you contrary and mean!" he shouted.

"Say what you want; I will not stay with Nurse Rebikov. I am going to America with you!" I shouted back at him.

Marina was in tears. "Olya, no one expected you to live, and we arranged for only five of us to go."

"I still will go whenever you go!" I screamed.

"I don't think it is possible now to get your name added," Lev said. "But I will go to see Grisha and do everything that can be done for you to come with us."

Instead of feeling happy and expressing my gratitude, I felt an overwhelming distrust for both of them, and ran outside, slamming the door.

It was so quiet. Even the birds, usually so busily noisy, were silent, and I realized that my heart was beating so loudly that I could hear the *thump, thump*. I walked past the vegetable garden, stopped at the cow barn, gazed at the trees and bushes where we gathered leaves and berries, and something happened to me. Mother was everywhere I looked, but when I put out my arms to touch her, she vanished. I stumbled about madly with outstretched arms until my feet crumbled under me. I was sprawled on the ground, the dry grass and bright-colored leaves cushioning my face, muting my sobs.

Would Father miss me if I did not come? Could he have told Lev to leave me here while the family went to America? I could not believe that. Papa's face appeared, soft, kind. Surely he loved me.

But why did they have to leave my name out? Couldn't they have waited for me to get well? Didn't they want me, because I was ugly and had no hair? I again touched the fuzz and felt for wisps on my head.

Father would understand, I thought. *I will have long plaits one day and Father will pull them and tease me as he used to!* I sat up, my knees under my chin, and then I heard a boisterous "Boo!" and found Sasha and Vera behind me.

"Where have you been?" Vera asked. "We have been hunting for you for a long time," she said.

"Why?" I asked in alarm.

"Lev sent us to look for you," Sasha said.

I suddenly felt cold. "Is anyone at the house—Nurse Rebikov?" I whispered.

Vera laughed. "No, why would she be there? No one is sick."

I stopped shaking and walked back to the house with them. Marina and Lev were at the table talking. They looked at me, and I suddenly felt such terror that I again started to tremble.

"Come, sit down." Lev pointed to a chair. I looked at Sasha and Vera on each side of me. I felt so alone that I needed them.

"Can they stay with me now?" I asked in a small voice.

Lev laughed. "No, Olya, I want to talk to you alone," he said, and told them to go out to play. Timidly, I took the chair next to his.

"Olya, it is all set. We will all escape to Poland the way Papa did."

Somehow the "all" in his statement didn't include me, and my pain and anger left me speechless. So that's why they wanted me—to justify leaving me!

"If you are going to tell me that I am to stay with the Rebikovs and that they will be good to me, stop! I won't do it. I am going to America with the rest of you!" I screamed.

Lev stared at me, and Marina held out her arms. "That's what we are trying to tell you!" She smiled at me happily. "Lev spoke to Grisha. It is all settled. You are to leave with us! Lev is waiting for a special paper to fill out for you in Poland."

Lies and more lies! I thought, feeling sick with rage, and avoided her outstretched arms.

"Olya." Lev smiled. "Did you think Father would allow us to come to America without you, or that we wanted to leave you?" he asked in a serious voice.

I burst into wild sobbing. Vitya, sitting in the chair next to me, cradled my head in her lap.

"Stop crying, Olya. We are all going to America!" she said happily.

I so wanted to believe that they were telling me the truth, but I couldn't.

24

GOD! HOW I needed to have the assurance that I, too, was to go to America, but I trusted neither Lev nor Marina. *They are trying to keep me quiet, less alert,* I thought, wondering if they had any idea of the turbulence within me. Every time I heard or thought I heard wheels on the road, my heart began to pound. I was sure that the Rebikovs were coming for me!

At night, I was afraid to fall asleep and clung to Vera. Part of me had to be touching her at all times. She was my security.

I trusted no one. When I came across Vitya surrounded by coats, I looked at her suspiciously.

"What are you doing?" I asked her. She turned to the table, put her hand into a large pile of clothing, and pulled out my old green jacket.

"I don't think it needs mending. All the buttons are on," I said.

Vitya's eyes sparkled. "You're right; I am not mending.

I am sewing something very special into each piece of our clothing."

"What?" I asked, almost smiling, because I remembered Parazka sewing things into our clothes to keep us from having colds and to keep evil spirits away. Vitya showed me a little white bag.

"What's in it?" I asked curiously.

"Something very precious." Vitya opened the bag and took out a ring with a large, bright stone. "It belongs to Papa. Sewn into our clothes, no one will know it is there, we won't be robbed, and when we are in other countries before getting to America, we can sell it and have money for food and other things." She picked up my jacket and started ripping the lining underneath the sleeve.

I stared at her and at the jacket. Old and worn, but it was mine! And for the first time I felt sure that I was not to be left behind. An overwhelming sense of relief and happiness filled me to overflowing. I threw my arms around Vitya and kissed her. She looked at me, her lovely brown eyes wide.

"You are better, Olya. You have not been yourself for so long. We were terribly worried," she said, hugging me.

"I'm well, all well!" I exclaimed, and suddenly burst into tears.

Lev jumped up. "What's the matter? Why are you crying?" he asked anxiously.

I smiled, blinking through my tears. "Because I'm so happy," I cried, kissing him on the cheek, and hurriedly ran to Marina, almost knocking her off her chair, and threw my arms about her.

"Olya! You are just as you were before you became sick." She smiled at me happily.

"And a good thing, too," Lev spoke up. "We leave very soon. Pray for good weather, Olya."

"I will, I will! It will be beautiful weather when we leave." I sang and danced about the room. Everyone laughed, and I climbed on my bed, feeling ecstatic, free of anger and doubt, but suddenly very tired. I slept through dinner, all night, and I was the one Vera had to wake the next morning!

The following days were busy and anxious, and the first question each morning was always "Is it today?"

Lev's voice often revealed his own anxiety and concern about the delay. "I'll tell you when I know" was all he would say. He looked older as he sat at the table, his brows knit, poring over maps with Vitya and Marina on each side of him.

"Go outside," they urged Vera, Sasha, and me, and we did not object. It was still warm, the treetops ablaze with color, and the low foliage, goldenrod, bright blue cornflowers, and the brilliant shades of bushes and weeds artfully mixed their colors, enjoying their last days together. Slow-moving, sleepy bees rested heavily on flowers, and an occasional butterfly crossed my view.

Would I ever see such beauty again? I wondered, and stopped in mid-thought, half ashamed. In America, of course! *Everything in America is always beautiful.* Yet I stood in our woods, filled with the beauty of the Russian autumn day, and felt like a bee who sucks the last of the nectar from a flower, feeling a strange pain in parting with it.

When Marina called us to come back for lunch, I was the last to come in, although I was very hungry. Lev was silent during lunch, preoccupied and unmistakably nervous. He left the table before we were finished eating, paced the floor, and came back to his seat.

"Today is the day! We leave late tonight," he said solemnly.

Instead of excitement, we took the news for which we had been waiting so long quietly. Now that the time had actually come for us to leave, we were both sad and very frightened.

"Do we walk?" Sasha found his voice.

"No, I will tell you about that later," Lev told him.

"What about Mama?" Vera said shakily. "Must she stay here?"

Lev reached for her hand. "Yes, Vera," he whispered hoarsely. "But," he continued, "we are all going to the cemetery to say good-bye to her."

As we entered the old worn cemetery gates, we walked knee-high through weeds and bushes, shrieking with brilliant colors, heightened by the afternoon sun.

"I am not at all sure where the grave is. I hope we can find it," Lev muttered with some uncertainty. I knew exactly where it was. Some unknown force led me to it, and the others followed. The whole grave was covered with color-drenched weeds, and Lev looked at me. "Is this it?" he asked. I moved the weeds aside and pointed to the board Yakov had left on the top. Vitya burst into tears and turned away. The rest of us stood with bowed heads, while Sasha's eyes nervously traveled over graves close by.

"Was Mama this little?" he suddenly asked, pointing to her grave. No one answered him, for none of us dared to speak. He continued looking at the grave, his eyes moving from one end to the other.

"She must be lonely here!" he said, and burst into tears. Marina reached for his hand, but he moved away, still looking intently at the grave. Walking to one end, he said, "I suppose this is the top of you, Mama." We stared as he got down on his knees, took the whistle out of his pocket, put it to his lips, blew it cautiously, and pushed it among the weeds. "This is for you, Mama. Blow it when you feel lonely." His last words were piercingly shrill, and we watched him running until he was out of the gate. Vitya started to follow him, but Lev caught her by the arm.

"He will be all right; leave him alone," he said, and reached into his upper pocket and pulled out a paper. We knew at once it was Parazka's letter for Mother. His voice was low, but clear, as he started to read.

" 'Sleep in peace, sleep warm, Anna Nikolayevna, child of my heart, light of my world. You left me four days before your thirty-sixth birthday.' " Lev wiped his eyes with the palm of his hand, bent down, and placed it next to Sasha's whistle.

Weeping was the only sound in the cemetery. Even the birds and wind were silent. Everyone was crying. I alone stood dry-eyed. All of me was with Mama, and it was hard to force myself to accept the fact that she was dead and that we were at her grave. Glimpses of her sweet, calm face surrounded by pink cherry blossoms kept flashing before me. Suddenly I knelt down and started digging at the dry earth with my nails, gathering bits of earth mingled with colorful weeds and placing them in my handkerchief, which I tied carefully and put in my pocket.

"To keep me ever close to you! Bye, Mama. I love you," I mouthed as we were leaving and I half expected to hear her say, "Good-bye, Olya. I love you, too."

Outside the gate, Sasha was crying quietly and made no move to follow us.

"Do you suppose he is sorry to have left his whistle?" Vitya asked quietly.

Lev turned to him. "Sasha, do you want your whistle back? I can get it in a minute."

"No!" Sasha screamed, and glared angrily at Lev. "I left it for Mama." Sasha again started to run. Marina caught up with him, and the two of them walked on ahead.

Just as on the day we buried her, we returned to our house in late afternoon and were greeted by a sunset of crimson gold. It was a cruel reminder, and it brought to the surface all the painful sadness and grief we had tried to overcome. Mother's bed in the far corner of the room was exactly as it had been that day, and I kept my eyes on it, expecting to see Mother in it. The room was so empty without her.

"Our last meal here!" Vitya said as she brought the food, which we ate in silence.

Lev searched our faces when the table was cleared. "Now I will tell you about our trip," he said. "We will go in a large wagon. It will take all night and most of tomorrow for us to get to the Polish border. From there we hope to go to America the way Papa did."

"Who will drive us?" Vera asked.

"Grisha!" Lev answered.

At the mention of Grisha's name, we became excited and started asking questions.

"Can I ride up front with Grisha?" Sasha pleaded.

"Escape means that we are to be hidden so that no one can see us, so you cannot ride on the seat with Grisha," Lev said.

"Why must we be hidden? Nobody is looking for us!" I cried.

Lev lowered his voice. "Koznikov would never give us the papers we need to leave the country, and I am sure he has warned all town officials between here and the Polish border to make sure that we do not escape," he said sadly.

"It will be scary, but fun!" Sasha's eyes were bright.

"Yes, scary, but also very dangerous for Grisha and for us all," Lev answered.

Marina and Vitya packed every scrap of bread or fruit not eaten and placed them into various bundles.

"This is for our trip," Marina said. Sasha started to say something, but Lev interrupted him.

"Now, listen carefully. We are to dress now in the clothes we will wear on the trip and go to bed dressed. Try to sleep until Grisha comes for us," Lev said.

"Sleep in our coats!" Sasha asked.

"Not in your coats, but don't even take off your shoes! Please try to sleep!" he said again.

We nodded, not feeling in the least sleepy.

"Now, the most important thing I have to tell you." Lev's voice sounded official. "When Grisha comes, he will tell us where he wants us in the wagon. You are to do exactly what he says!"

It was very exciting but very frightening, and before it was dark, Sasha was in Lev's bed, and Vera and I whispered to each other under our blanket until she fell asleep. I stayed awake, watching Lev, Marina, and Vitya checking bundles, putting things away, and I smiled in my utter happiness. I was not to be left with the Rebikovs! America! How wonderful to be going to America! My eyes traveled over the room and I could see Mama's bed even in the dim light. My mind knew we would go without her, but something inside me was smoldering, filling me with a painful sadness. I wondered how Papa would receive us without Mama. My eyes moved to the windows and my thoughts turned to the cherry trees. I would never again see them in bloom. Parazka! We would leave without saying good-bye to her. Grisha—I smiled sadly. We would be with him, yet so far apart. I started to imagine the fun we would have if we could ride with him, laugh, sing, eat together; but this was not to be. My mind raced, sadness enveloping me like a thick fog, overshadowing the folds of happiness, of the joy I had felt earlier because I, too, was going to America.

25

VITYA GRABBED ME by both shoulders and shook me angrily. I sat up, rubbing my eyes. She shook me again, and Lev's angry voice came across the room in a loud whisper. "Get moving! Get Vera up!" His voice penetrated my sleepy stupor. I got off the bed and started tugging at Vera. She slept no matter how hard I pulled her arm or shook her. I glared at her angrily, took hold of one of her plaits, and pulled with all my might. Vera let out a sharp scream and sat up very suddenly. Lev was at our bed instantly, and putting one hand over her mouth, he shook me hard with the other.

"What's the matter with you? You're stupid to act like this now!" he hissed angrily. "Get some sense or . . ." He gritted his teeth and let go of me so suddenly that I sprawled to the floor, fully awake now, hot tears of surprise and hurt filling my eyes.

A shadow appeared and a large gentle hand pulled me up.

"Grisha!" I whispered joyously, forgetting my tears. He gave me a loving squeeze.

"Let's see what I can do with Vera," he whispered, and hugged her. Within minutes she and I had dressed and smoothed our hair. Lev urged Sasha toward us.

"You three sit on this bed without making a sound," he snapped. We obeyed, not daring to move. *Why is Lev so angry?* I wondered. *Can he boss us now because he is in charge? Perhaps he's frightened!* Neither Papa nor Mama had ever been so sharp with us!

I tried but could not see his face. The only light in the house came from a single candle on the table, and I realized that the windows were covered with bedspreads or quilts. I don't know how long we sat before Lev told us to come to the table where Grisha and my older sisters were seated. Grisha looked very serious and spoke in a loud whisper.

"Since you have no permission to leave the country, I will help you escape. I need your complete cooperation."

"You can depend on us," Lev said emphatically.

"Once I get you across the border into Poland, you will be safe. Koznikov will no longer be able to hurt you, and from there you will find your way to America."

"Will you come with us?" Sasha asked, trying hard to quiet his excited voice.

"Let's cross the border first," Grisha told him.

"Will we go in your wagon?" Vera asked. Grisha scratched his head.

"Yes. It is a large wagon. My father and I worked long to build it so you can be in it without being seen."

"Magic!" Sasha cried, and Grisha put his finger to his mouth.

"I must tell you about it. The wagon has two parts,"

he said, and seeing our puzzled expression, paused, searching for words to describe it.

"It is like—like bunk beds! The top will be full of straw and other things, and the lower part is where you will be hidden. There is a sliding door to allow you to get in and out easily, and Dumka put in blankets and pillows for you."

"Do we have to sleep all the time?" Vera asked timidly.

"No, Vera, but I'm afraid that because it is so low, you will have to stay flat on your side or back most of the time. Maybe Sasha, because he is small, will be able to sit up, but the rest of you would bump your heads," he said regretfully. There was a long pause. We were thinking, imagining the trip to the border.

"How will we go to the toilet?" I asked, feeling both puzzled and embarrassed.

"Olya, I will stop in the woods anytime I think it is safe. When I slide the door open, you can get out to stretch and use the woods as your toilet."

"Will we have any food?" Vera now asked in a frightened voice.

"No more questions! Of course we will all have food, silly," Lev snapped and turned to Grisha.

"Anything else you need to tell us?"

"Yes, something very important. Listen carefully. The success of this trip depends on your doing exactly as you are told—mostly, to be very quiet!"

"You mean we can't even whisper?" I braved Lev's ire to ask.

Grisha's laugh was comforting. "There will be many times during our journey when you will be able to talk and sing, if you want to, but I will tell you when." He stopped and gave a low chuckle. "When I talk or sing to my horses,

I will be telling you something. Remember when I tell the horses they are noisy, you are to be absolutely silent. This is important," he said. "Are we ready?"

"One minute," Marina said, and she and Vitya handed small parcels wrapped in cloth to Vera, Sasha, and me. "Hold on to these!" Marina told us.

"I can carry more," I volunteered.

"You won't need to. This is your food. Remember, keep this near you in the wagon," she said.

"Ready?" Lev asked nervously and suddenly cried, "To the toilet everybody." Two by two we left the house to go to the back of the stable, and when we were all together again, Lev said, "Ready!"

It was pitch dark, and we nervously followed him to the wagon on the back road. We felt, rather than saw, him slide a large board-like door upward, but we could see nothing but a black pit, where we were to spend our last hours in our country.

"You must feel your way in and find a place. When it gets light, you will be able to see through some small holes we put in, and you will be able to make yourselves more comfortable," Grisha whispered to us. Lev and Sasha climbed in first, Vitya and Vera followed, and Marina and I were last. We crawled over the others to find a spot to lie in.

"I hope we can breathe," Marina whispered.

"It's so black in here. I'm scared," I whispered.

"Settle down. We'll be all right." Lev spoke unsympathetically.

"All in?" Grisha's voice was close.

"All in," Lev told him, and Grisha lowered the door.

"It's like being buried!" I moved closer to Marina, and soon we felt the wheels slowly moving under us. Huddled close to each other, we often found someone's arm or leg in our faces, but despite discomfort, the rhythmic rocking soon lulled us back to sleep.

When I awoke, Lev was looking out through a small hole.

"Still dark," he whispered, "but we are moving on. By this evening, we will be across the border, really on our way to America."

"I hope we can stop before it gets light," Marina said.

"So do I," Vitya whispered. Both sounded uncomfortable.

"Grisha will . . ." Lev started to talk, but stopped suddenly. Other sounds now began to mingle with those of the creaks and groans of the wagon wheels, and then we heard voices. The wagon came to a full stop, and we heard Grisha say, "And a good morning to you, comrade!"

"Where to?" a man's deep voice asked. There was a second of silence during which our hearts beat wildly, and then Grisha's laugh.

"Going to pick up the wife in the next village. She's been visiting her mother." The wagon gave a lurch, but Grisha held fast to the reins.

"Go on, you may pass, but I'm sure you're in no hurry," the man's voice followed him. Grisha laughed and we relaxed.

The wheels were now gaining speed and above the wagon noise we heard Vera's sullen voice, "I'm hungry!"

"Get your package I gave you when we left. Food's in it," Vitya whispered to her.

We all started searching for our food parcels, and flat on our backs or on our sides, we chewed the bread and dried fruit slowly.

Vera raised her head slightly. "No tea?" she whispered. "I'm thirsty."

"No, Vera, no tea," Marina told her.

"I'm all dry. I want something to drink," she pleaded.

"Stop it at once!" Lev ordered, but Vera's whimpers turned to sobs. "If you don't stop it, I'll smack you!" Lev threatened.

Vera became silent like the rest of us, but our discomfort and irritability increased.

Then the wagon made a sudden lurch and stopped.

"Lord, I hope this is a rest!" Vitya said.

"Silence!" Lev whispered, and I could see his hand in front of his mouth cautioning us to be very still.

The horses snorted, and we heard Grisha talking to them softly, then footsteps coming from a distance, walking on a hard surface. We strained our ears. Where were we? What was happening? Were we going to stop? Then we heard a woman's voice, cold, official.

"Where to? State your business, comrade."

"Zdolbunov to get the wife, visiting her sick mother." Grisha's voice again sounded tired.

"Your papers, comrade." There was a long silence, and we knew Grisha was going through his pockets, searching the way he always did when he had to produce a receipt or list. We prayed that he had them.

"Here, comrade!" came Grisha's relieved voice.

"How long will you be in the village?" she asked.

"Not long. It all depends on her mother. I might even have to go home without her if the old *babushka* is still sick."

"What's in the wagon?"

"Not much of anything. Some hay for the horses, for me to nap in."

"Sure of that?" she questioned again.

"Some food for me and these poor beasts." There was a puzzling silence, and our stomachs turned sick.

"Pass!" came her voice of ice, and we wished we could see Grisha's face. We knew he'd be smiling.

The wagon started with a slow grind, the wheels creaking as if in complaint of the horrible ditches in the mud roads.

"I wonder where we are," Marina whispered. Lev again peered through a small hole.

"Can't see a thing—woods, but it's light!"

"That means a long wait before we can get out?" Vitya whispered in a discouraged voice.

"Can't tell," Lev said irritably. "I'm so cramped, I don't think I could walk even if we did stop," he said miserably. Although no one else said anything, we all felt the same as we bounced along on the floor of the wagon.

A cry from Sasha shattered the stillness. "I need to pee," followed momentarily by, "I'm wet! My trousers are wet!" Grisha started to hum loudly.

"Don't worry, Sasha. We are . . ." Grisha's loud humming stopped Marina from finishing her sentence. His humming now changed to singing, and we recognized a song Mother had taught us about a frightened little rabbit. We listened carefully. The tune we knew well, but the words he sang distinctly over and over were different.

"Little rabbits are safe from the dogs of the hunters only when they are still so the dogs can't find them."

"We are moving. Why is he telling us to be quiet?" Lev whispered. "We must be nearing inspection. Grisha is warning us. Not a sound!"

Grisha continued singing, and we felt the wagon slowing down and again come to a sudden halt.

It was a noisy place where he stopped. Voices, other wagons groaning and screeching, discontented horses, wagons stopping and moving on, and the smell of horse manure came at us like sudden smoke out of a clogged chimney. We held our breaths, hoped Grisha would move and get us away from the familiar yet objectionable smell, but there was neither sound nor movement from him.

What's happened to him? Our fright almost turned to panic.

Where were we? How much longer were we to remain hidden in the dark bowels of the wagon, not daring to talk or move? Suddenly, a voice close to our wagon shouted, "Move to the left, comrade." Our wagon moved over.

"Papers!" This time Grisha had them ready, and again the same questions.

"Alone? Where to?" and Grisha told them.

"Anything in the wagon?"

"Yes, hay, straw, some food," Grisha replied.

"Sure you're not smuggling anyone across the border? We have a list!" someone shouted, and we heard the shuffling of paper.

Grisha's reply was one of his hearty laughs. "The only thing I'd like to smuggle or push across the border—or—" Grisha stopped—"is my mother-in-law. She's forever asking for help!" He laughed again.

"Search the wagon!" someone shouted. "If someone is hidden in the hay, tell us now. We search with sharp pitchforks!" the speaker warned.

We froze, crouched as low as we could, our hands moved across our heads and faces to protect them from the pitchfork. Vera moaned and fought Vitya's hand quickly placed over her mouth. Suddenly a man's voice exclaimed, "Now, what's this?" We were sure that we had been discovered, and waited, resigned, almost relieved, for the door to open, for us to be dragged out. Perspiration like salt tears began to run down our faces as we lay flat, limp, and helpless. We even became impatient for the door to open.

What are they waiting for?

Grisha's voice shocked us back to the living.

"This?" Grisha laughed his hearty laugh. "The last of the vodka, comrade. You can't blame me for taking a nip now and then. It's a long, lonely trip. But there's a full bottle for my wife's old man. I rather like him."

A conversation followed that we could not understand, and we did not care. We were trying to put ourselves together again.

We were not caught! Maybe we'll make it!

"All right, comrade. The town you want is close by; follow the road to the right from here," someone shouted.

"Thank you, comrades!" Grisha's voice came through to us. We could feel his pull on the reins, and the wagon reeled forward again with a sigh.

Grisha instantly started to sing different words to our rabbit tune.

"Sing softly, if you are good, or you'll wake your grandmother and then you'll get it."

"That means we can talk?" I whispered.

"Yes," Lev said, and we started whispering to each other.

Sasha started to cry.

"I know you're wet and uncomfortable, Sasha," Lev told him, "but don't worry. You're not the only one," he said.

"If only we could stop!" Marina was in tears. "Maybe we could get rid of some of the terrible stench in the wagon as well."

"I'm going to try something," Lev said, looking through one of the small holes. "Nothing but woods," he said, scrambling over us to the very front of the wagon. "This is where Grisha sits," he whispered. "I'm going to bang my fists and try to get his attention. Perhaps we could stop," he said, beating at the seat with his fists. There was no response and Lev banged again, but still no sign that Grisha heard him.

"I suppose it's not safe," he said miserably, and we all wriggled in our discomfort.

The horses plodded along, their hooves maintaining the same tired rhythmic beat, when suddenly it changed, and we felt the wagon make a rather sharp turn and stop. The horses seemed relieved and made appropriate noises, and we heard Grisha talking to them softly.

"Poor beasts. You must be tired and hungry. I'll give you a rest and some food." We knew he was unharnessing the horses and could imagine them shaking themselves and enjoying their freedom.

"What about us?" Lev whispered. "We are tired, too!" We prayed he would soon open our door and free us briefly from our prison. We were impatient, frantic until we heard a scratching on the door followed by Grisha's loud whisper.

"You can't all come out at once. Two by two when I open the door."

There was a slight delay, and we knew Grisha was checking to make sure it was safe, and then he swiftly raised the door. The fresh air that came at us was so wonderful! I felt like a fish, moving my mouth to breathe in the cool air.

"The two out must be very careful. If you see anyone with me as you come back, hide until I call you. Understand?" he asked, and helped Vera and Vitya out. Poor

Vitya could barely walk and leaned on Vera as they disappeared into the thicket. Grisha had shut the door again, and we waited impatiently for him to open it. When he did, Sasha and Lev stumbled out and limped to the woods. When they climbed back, Marina and I got out, slowly, painfully.

All too soon we were once more on our way. Our determination to save our food did not last long. We ate bits of bread and fruit from our parcels sporadically, but time passed slowly.

"I think it's only about two hours now to the border. Grisha must be exhausted!" Lev said. But when Grisha began to sing, he did not sound in the least fatigued. The melody, so familiar, filtered down to us from his seat above.

"Little rabbit do beware, the hunters' dogs are almost there!"

"We must be close to the Polish border," Lev whispered. "Remember, as soon as Grisha opens the door, I'll be the first out. Jump right after me and run as fast as you can. Follow me. Don't look back. Keep running until we are across all the railway tracks. To the right there is a large clump of birch trees and bushes. We will hide there!"

"Will Grisha come with us?" Sasha asked.

"I don't think so, Sasha. Just do as you are told. Remember, we must be absolutely still when Grisha warns us to be quiet."

"Can't we even kiss Grisha good-bye?" Vera was in tears and Lev almost spat the words at her.

"No, Vera, just do as you're told!"

Vera cried in a low voice, and the wagon became a very active place.

"Find your jacket. If you are not wearing it, get it on," Vitya's whisper was crisp and urgent.

182

"All jackets on?" Marina checked. "Take any food left in your parcel," she reminded us.

"Remember, as soon as the panel is open and Lev is out, the person closest to the door must jump and follow Lev. Run! *Don't stop*, no matter what!" Vitya repeated Lev's instructions.

Trembling with fear and excitement, we stayed flat on our backs, clutching our parcels. The horses, despite their brief rest, seemed to feel their burden and moved with less vigor. Lev twisted his head to look out the hole closest to him.

"Still not quite dark. Grisha said we'd get to the border just as it was getting dark." He sounded puzzled.

"I see—" he started to say but was interrupted by Grisha's singing.

"Little rabbits do beware, hunters' dogs are everywhere," he sang in a loud lilting, almost childish voice. We understood his warning.

Then we heard an angry male voice.

"What makes you so happy? Where do you think you are going?" The wagon stopped.

"What's this place, comrade?" Grisha's voice did not sound like him, and his speech was thick and slurred. We froze with fear. What was wrong? He sounded different, so awful!

"You are at the Polish border. Where are you going?" another angry voice cried out.

"I'm to get—I'm to get—I remember now. I'm to pick up—" He stopped. "I'm to take my wife home."

"Where is your wife?"

"Now, let me see—a village near here. But I forgot the name."

"Comrade, you're drunk or daffy, and maybe both. How

will you get her if you don't know the name of the village?"
Grisha roared with laughter.

"I know, I know. It is—Zelov? No! Zebulov? I got it,
Zebulov!" Grisha shouted triumphantly.

"He's dead drunk!" came a man's voice. "He means
Zdolbunov!"

"That's it! How clever I am!" Grisha shouted gleefully.

"If you are looking for Zdolbunov, you have passed it
a long time ago."

"What do I do now?" Grisha asked, yawning loudly.

Our very bones froze with fright. What could have
happened to him? Had he forgotten about us? Was he really
drunk? These questions flew through our minds, our panic
increasing with his every utterance.

"Pull your wagon to the side and get some sleep, you
damn drunk!" someone shouted.

The wagon did not budge. We heard things above us
shuffling, Grisha's heavy footsteps, and then his uproarious
laughter as he shouted, "Here, comrades! A full bottle of
vodka. I'd rather drink it with you than give it to the wife's
old man!"

We felt his weight against the door of our escape and
held our breaths. On our backs, jackets on, bundles in our
hands, we waited and listened to Grisha and the two guards.

"Come on, be good fellows. Drink with me. Soon I
have to face my wife and her mother. Do have a drink with
me—it will sober me up!" Grisha begged. There was laughter, and we knew some of the guards had come closer to
the wagon. We froze with fear when we felt the door slowly
moving upward.

"He is going to hand us over to the guards!" Lev
whispered in terror.

Then came Grisha's voice. "If we drink here, we're sure to be seen. Come, let's go to the other side! No one will see us there!" he said thickly. "Come to the other side—come—drink with me!" he coaxed.

We heard his ponderous drunken walk and the snickering laughter of the guards. "He's really too drunk to go on," one of them said, and we knew they were following Grisha's steps to the other side of the wagon.

Lev suddenly moved like lightning, quietly pushing the panel door up, and catlike, he slid down, holding out his arms to Sasha and Vera, and then started to run toward the railway tracks. We followed blindly as if we were somehow connected by the springs of a machine, all working together, down a steep grassy incline, our legs moving in unison across the tracks, deep high grassy patches, until we reached the clump of birch trees and heavy bushes. We collapsed, out of breath, dirty rivulets of perspiration running down our faces. Our minds immediately turned across the tracks—*Grisha!*—and we heard his voice, boisterous, drunken, still urging the guards to drink.

"Nothing like vodka, comrades, especially when you're on your way for the wife!"

"He's drunk, but otherwise fine!" Lev cried. "And because of him we are in Poland! Free!" he said.

Our eyes and ears were focused on the wagon, trying to see or hear what was going on, but we could see nothing. Soon he and the guards returned to the escape side of the wagon facing us. We stared at Grisha. He was really drunk, staggering, laughing, clowning like a big bear in the circus.

"Better get some sleep!" one of the guards told him.

"No, the vodka sobered me up! I'd better get going or the wife will clobber me!" he replied in his big booming voice.

"Do as you wish, comrade, but don't forget where you're going—Zdolbunov. Don't get lost again!" someone shouted.

"I wouldn't mind getting lost or staying here if you had more vodka!" he roared.

"It was your vodka—you're really drunk!"

"Who cares! Good reinforcement for meeting the wife," Grisha answered thickly.

We watched him climb on to his seat clumsily. Vitya was on her feet ready to run back, Sasha at her heels, but Lev grabbed them both and pushed them down to the grass. "Are you crazy?"

"Grisha! Grisha!" Marina shouted.

"Sh-sh." Lev pushed her down angrily. "Do you want him shot?"

We were silent at once, holding back our sobs with great difficulty. As the wagon began to move, Grisha called, "Good-bye, comrades, good-bye, comrade Commandant, good-bye, my very dear friends." His voice grew faint, and we kept our eyes on the slow-moving vehicle until it was out of sight.

"Are we going to sleep here?" Sasha's voice broke the silence.

"No, Sasha, we are to wait here. Someone will come to tell us what to do next!" Marina said. Sasha put his head on her lap and was soon asleep. We listened to the strange sounds above us in the trees, the whistling of trains in the distance, but all was quiet across the railway tracks.

"I hope whoever is to meet us will come soon!" Marina spoke unhappily.

"They will! They will!" Lev said, but his voice lacked conviction.

26

IT WAS STRANGE that we neither heard them nor saw the dim light of their lantern until they were right across the road from us. We jumped up and stood close together, trying to make out the approaching forms. There were two of them.

"Koshansky?" a man's low voice asked. We were suddenly very frightened and did not answer. Could it be Koznikov after us?

"Don't be afraid," the same voice said in Russian. "We're to meet you and put you on a train for Rovno."

We relaxed. "Are we glad you are here! We were getting worried!" Lev cried.

"You got here earlier than we expected; sorry if we gave you a scare!" The man's voice was gentler.

"No matter; you came. Where to now?" Lev asked.

There was a low chuckle from the man, not a sound from the person with him. "First we must pass through the Polish border guards and then . . ."

"Then what?" Lev sounded scared.

"Don't worry a bit. There are no problems, only a formality—you are safe." He stopped and laughed. "Sorry, I should have introduced myself. I am Steffan Mieszkowski. This is my wife, Mia," and for the first time we realized that the second person was a woman. We couldn't see either one clearly, but Mrs. Mieszkowski raised the lantern to have a better look at us. We blinked in the dim light and saw a slim blond woman.

"Steffan, they are so young," she murmured.

"Yes, they are! We must do all we can to help them," her husband said. "Let's get to our wagon down the road," he added and started to walk. We followed the small circle of light shed by the lantern Mrs. Mieszkowski was carrying. She tried to take Sasha's hand, but he moved closer to Vitya and held on to her hand tightly.

Mrs. Mieszkowski stopped. "You must be starved and tired, but we'll soon take care of that."

The Mieszkowski wagon was as large as Grisha's. Mr. Mieszkowski helped us into the back, and he and his wife sat up front. We made ourselves comfortable in the fresh-smelling hay, and the horses moved along at a brisk pace. We did not talk. Vera and Sasha, their heads cradled in Vitya's and Marina's laps, fell asleep. When we stopped before a small, dim-lit building, Steffan Mieszkowski jumped off, helped his wife down, and both reached to help us climb out of the wagon.

The door of the building suddenly opened, casting a triangle of light around us. A uniformed guard asked for papers, which were immediately produced. He peered at us, counted us one by one without saying a word, and feeling relieved, we climbed back into the wagon.

"Are we going to the station for our train?" Lev asked.

"Heavens, no! There is no train for Rovno until to-morrow evening. We are taking you to our house for the night," Mrs. Mieszkowski told us. "Maybe we can wash some of your clothes before you leave," she added, and we realized that both we and our clothes were much in need of scrubbing.

The Mieszkowski house was almost a replica of the cottage we had left, only it was bigger. The lamp in the center of the square wooden table lit up the room, and as we looked around, we knew that they were not rich, yet when Mrs. Mieszkowski brought food to the table, we were amazed. Meat, vegetables, and milk! We had not realized how hungry we were and ate ravenously. Our hosts watched us and urged us to eat more. Even Vera stretched in her seat and said, "No, thank you!" when another potato was placed on her plate.

"Now for bed!" Mrs. Mieszkowski said, smiling at Sasha. "Girls, come with me," she called, opening a door into a small dark room. She quickly lit a lamp, and we saw one large bed and one straw mattress on the floor. "This should be enough," she said.

"Are we taking your bed?" Marina was distressed. Mrs. Mieszkowski laughed.

"No, Steffan and I have our own bed. . . ." She suddenly changed the subject. "Take your clothes off. They need to be washed—at least some of them do. I'm heating water."

We were too tired to argue that we could wash our own clothes; we were soon fast asleep.

The next day, bundled in some of the clothes of the Mieszkowskis while ours were drying in the swift cool wind, we had an early breakfast, feeling as if we had always known them. When Steffan Mieszkowski had to leave for work, he shook hands with Lev, hugged the rest of us, and lifting Sasha way up into the air, cried, "You're in charge now— take care of things!" Sasha grinned widely. He was so happy! We were all more comfortable than we could remember. Marina and Vitya helped with the cooking. We felt at home, carefree, and laughed when we saw the huge kettles of water on the stove.

"For your baths," said Mia Mieszkowski, and we all had a much-needed scrubbing.

"My, you look clean and pretty." Mrs. Mieszkowski beamed at us. It was such a luxury for us to be clean, in clothes smelling of wind and sun. It was also good to see Vera and Sasha so contentedly following Mrs. Mieszkowski about like pet puppies.

We were so happy that we gave little thought to our impending journey until early afternoon, when Steffan Mieszkowski returned. Sasha ran to him almost as he used to do when Papa came home. Lev and Steffan Mieszkowski left us outside, and they sat indoors, talking and looking at papers.

Then Steffan Mieszkowski called out, "Come, time to go!" and his wife appeared with a large bundle.

"Food for your trip!" She handed it to Lev. We stood, trying to keep the tears from spilling over, and could not find words to thank them.

There was a railway station in the town where the Mieszkowskis lived, even though it was as small as Sudilkov. Inside the building there were wooden benches for travelers to rest while waiting for trains. I was impressed, and I felt guilty for thinking the town in Poland was better than Sudilkov, so I immediately decided my town was better. I was mixed up, and my feelings of disloyalty, excitement, and fear reached my very bones! This was the first time since we left home that I allowed myself to think of Sudilkov, Papa, and America. *How much longer before we are in America, before we see him?* I wondered. Mia Mieszkowski put her hand on my shoulder, and I threw my arms about her and cried. Here, with the Mieszkowskis, I felt so secure, so at peace. I was ashamed for feeling the way I did, yet fear of the unknown, so exciting, had now become a frightening question mark.

Steffan Mieszkowski was again talking seriously to Lev. "Tickets for the trip all the way to Warsaw." He pointed to an envelope in his hand. "Remember, you get off in Rovno. There you wait two hours for a train to Lublin. In Lublin, you have a five-hour wait for a train to Warsaw, and I think someone will meet you at the station in Warsaw. Clear?" He handed Lev an envelope. "Keep it where you can get to it. Watch your money and tickets. Most people are good, but you never know—be cautious."

"I'll be careful; I'd better be!" Lev replied seriously.

"You'll be fine—all of you." Steffan Mieszkowski smiled.

Lev nodded, and as I watched him, I knew he, too, was frightened and apprehensive. We stood silently and waited nervously for the approaching train, which was blowing out huge circles of steam. Hugs and kisses and more hugs were exchanged, and as we mounted the platform to wave, Mia Mieszkowski was crying.

"Take care! Be careful!" they called as the train started to move.

We waved until they were out of sight before looking for seats.

27

WEARY, UNWASHED, AND frightened, we looked out the blurred train windows on the last lap of the journey to Warsaw. Five days and nights had passed since we had said good-bye to the Mieszkowskis. It seemed more like five weeks! Days and nights spent on crowded trains or sleeping on the floors of railway stations because of delays. We were used to discomfort, cold, and hunger, but it was not until both Vitya's and Sasha's coats were stolen that we experienced a new kind of panic. As Vitya wept, we wondered which of Mother's jewels sewn in the coats were lost. The excitement and joy of finally reaching Warsaw was gone.

Warsaw station was the biggest we had ever seen. It was crowded with people rushing about in all directions. We held hands and walked one behind the other like elephants holding on to each other's tails, at the same time searching people's faces.

"Someone is supposed to meet us," Lev said nervously.

"How would this someone know us?" Vitya looked at the throngs of people.

"There are six of us, together—I think they will . . ." He stopped as a tall young woman in a black fur jacket stood before us.

"Are you the Koshanskys?" she asked, looking at us intently, counting us, her eyes moving from one to the next.

Lev pulled us close to him. "Please tell us who you are and what you want with the Koshanskys." Surprised, the young woman laughed.

"Good! I'm glad you are cautious, and I am glad you finally arrived!" She smiled. "My name is Ann Polanski. I work for the HIAS. It is my job to meet immigrants arriving in Warsaw and find places for them to live and help in any way I can," she said.

"But we're not going to live in Warsaw; we are going to America!" Lev was alarmed. Ann Polanski smiled at him.

"I fear there will be a long wait before you get to America," she said. Opening a large bag, she took out a card and handed it to Lev. "Here is the card with the address of the HIAS. You are to come to this address to-morrow. We will advise you as to the necessary steps to get you to your father in America." Lev stared at the card.

"HIAS." He pronounced the word carefully. "Is this the organization that arranged for us to leave Russia and cross the border into Poland?" he asked.

"Possibly." Ann Polanski sounded tired and a bit impatient.

"What does HIAS mean?" Lev asked her.

"The letters in the word stand for Hebrew Immigration Aid Society. We help people who have to leave their country and we guide them to wherever they are going." She looked at her wristwatch. "It's late. Let's go," she said, and we all followed meekly.

When we got off the tram she led us into a large, square cobblestone courtyard. Tall buildings surrounded it, each merging into the other. We stared at the gray cobblestones and gray buildings, and way up high above the building there was the gray sky. There was not a single tree or bush in sight.

"It's like being inside a tall box," I thought out loud.

"These cobblestones are hundreds of years old," said Ann Polanski. "Some of the buildings also are old, but many have been expanded and changed. You will be in Building K." She opened a grimy, heavy gray door, and suddenly we were engulfed by a musty, sour smell that remained indelibly imprinted in my memory long after we left Building K.

Ann Polanski climbed the steep steps with great agility, and we huffed and puffed behind her. Out of breath, we finally stopped on the sixth floor. She consulted a little notebook, and soon we stood nervously at the door of the apartment which was to be our temporary home.

We followed Ann Polanski into a large dark room with small wooden chairs all around the walls. "The living room," she said, and she led us through a long dark hall and stopped before a door at the end. She knocked and opened it without waiting for a reply. "This is the room you are to share with the Danskers." She said good-bye and closed the door behind us, and we blinked in the dim light. We saw that the small room was divided by a dirty nondescript-colored curtain.

"Come, don't be upset!" A man spoke, and we realized we were not alone. "I'm Emil Dansker. This is my wife, and our children, Dena and Franz." He moved his arm toward a pale young woman and a girl about my age and her older brother.

"One small room for two families?" Lev asked angrily. "Where do we sleep?"

"On the floor, here in your part of the room," Mrs. Dansker told him. There were no windows in our part of the room. We looked at the four chairs against the walls, and Mr. Dansker quickly produced two others from his side of the curtain.

"We borrowed them last night—you weren't here—" he said apologetically.

We sat down heavily on the creaking chairs, and the Danskers disappeared.

"This will only be for a short time—come, it's not that bad!" said Vitya, trying to sound cheerful. Mrs. Dansker's head appeared from behind the curtain.

"Bedding is behind the door."

"What door?" we wondered, and realized that we were the lucky ones. The Danskers had a window, but we had a cupboard. Lev opened it and a bundle of quilts and pillows fell out. They were not clean. The odor of unwashed bodies and sweat clung to them.

"We can't use those!" Marina grimaced. Again Mrs. Dansker's head appeared from a small parting of the curtain.

"I know how you feel—but there's nothing you can do—we know!" she said sadly.

"How long have you been here?" Lev asked. There was a small pause.

"This is our eighth week," she answered.

We were shocked. Eight weeks! We expected to arrive in America in less than a month. Vitya burst into loud sobs. The curtain flew open and all the Danskers came out.

"We have been here a long time; perhaps we can keep you from making our mistakes," said Emil Dansker sympathetically. "This is the best there is for us. There are many Jews here waiting for help from the HIAS to get them to America."

"If only we could wash these before using them," Marina complained, pointing to the foul-smelling bedding.

Mrs. Dansker laughed bitterly. "That's an utter impossibility! There's only one bathroom."

"Can we use the kitchen sink for washing things?" Marina asked hopefully.

Mr. Dansker turned to his wife. "You should have told her we aren't allowed in the kitchen!"

"But where do we cook?" Vitya's voice was shrill.

"You don't cook. You eat what the landlord cooks for you and pay for it," Mrs. Dansker said angrily.

"Where is the dining room?" Lev asked.

"Right here. You eat sitting on your comfortable elegant chairs." Mrs. Dansker pointed to the wooden folding chairs, and Marina burst into tears. Mrs. Dansker patted her shoulder. "Don't take it so hard. You'll get used to it. We did, and all the others in this apartment."

"Are there others besides, living here?" Lev asked.

The Danskers sighed and Mr. Dansker explained. "There are four bedrooms in this apartment. The landlord uses one. There are twenty-four to thirty people sharing the other three bedrooms. Here in this room are ten of us. Ten of us sharing one room!"

"Couldn't we go elsewhere?" Vitya asked.

Mr. Dansker shook his head sadly. "There's not a thing we can do to change matters! Better get settled," he suggested.

We had a miserable night, sleeping in our clothes under

dirty blankets with our heads on stiff rubbery pillows. The next morning the Danskers led us into the living room, where we had a meager breakfast of thin slices of black bread with mugs of tea or watery soup.

Angry and discouraged, Lev went to the HIAS office and we waited for him on the hard chairs in the living room. He came back just as disheartened.

"What happened?" Marina asked.

"They will let Papa know we are in Poland, and ask him to send money for our boat passage from Belgium," he told us.

"You're silly to be so upset," Vitya told him.

"It shouldn't take too long and we will soon be on our way!" Marina tried to sound cheerful.

The HIAS office had asked Lev to wait a week before coming back, and when he did, he was told to be patient; there was no word as yet from Papa.

"Even when you get your money, you still must wait for your visas. Warsaw is full of people like you waiting to get out, and visas are given in order of application."

It was a blow to learn of the difficulties awaiting us, yet we could not develop greater patience and found it very hard to accept the advice of the kind, well-meaning occupants living with us in the apartment.

As days turned into weeks and there was still no word from Papa, we became more and more despondent. The weekly bills for our miserable food and lodging grew larger.

Lev was angry. "Last week it was about thirty percent less," he cried. "We took less food this week, yet it is so much more!"

We spent all the money Lev had brought into Poland in a short time, and Lev was forced to rip his own sleeve jacket to get the gold pendant with a large diamond in the center—Mama's pendant—which he sold. When he showed us the bag full of paper bills, Marina cried, "This should keep us for a long time."

"Not if we have to pay so much for our food and for this wretched place," Lev said unhappily.

Mrs. Dansker's voice from her side of the curtain interrupted him. "May I talk to you a minute?" she asked, stepping out to our side. She had her coat on, a heavy shawl over her head. "I couldn't help hearing what you said. Would you like to come to the station and buy bread as we do?" she asked.

"Can we do that?" Marina asked.

"Of course you can!" Mrs. Dansker's dark eyes were on the door. "Several of the Warsaw railway stations have stalls where bread and other things are sold. It is much cheaper than buying bread here by the slice!"

"Anything to save money!" Lev cried. "Vitya needs a coat; we all need clothes!"

"Don't be so self-conscious. We all smell the same; we stink!" Mrs. Dansker made a face. "Get your coats," she said, and Lev and Marina walked out with her.

Late in the afternoon they were back and were each carrying a paper sack. "You see, the bread was expensive, but nothing like what you pay here!" Mrs. Dansker said, disappearing behind her side of the curtain.

The bread was coarse and felt gritty between our teeth. "I'll bet the bakers add sand to the flour to make it weigh more," said Vitya.

Lev chewed slowly. "It's not any different from the bread we get here, and . . ." He turned to the corner where he had left the bags. He said, "Something special," and produced a large chunk of yellow cheese.

"May we have some, please? We want some!" Vera and Sasha cried.

"Yes, we can each have a small slice."

Four weeks after the sale of Mother's pendant, Lev again returned from the office of the HIAS. He was elated. Papa had sent the money for our tickets. The passports were ready.

"When do we leave?" we cried excitedly.

"Now we must wait for visas," Lev answered.

"Will it take long?" Vitya asked.

"It shouldn't," Lev said. "Soon we'll be on our way!"

He was wrong. We waited and waited. There was no end of red tape, and lining up for hours at a time became a daily ritual for Lev. Each day he returned more discouraged. We were all disheartened, bored, and very angry.

Though we did manage to get a coat for Vitya because she could not go out otherwise, we bought very little else. Everything was so expensive! We had no change of clothes and couldn't stand ourselves or each other. There was no way we could possibly be clean, and the stench of the hallways and stairs clung to us.

Finally after we had been in Warsaw ten weeks, we had our visas! "We really are on our way!" Lev cried.

Ann Polanski came to make final arrangements for our departure. "It's simply wonderful and calls for a celebration!" she said, handing Marina a package.

Marina blushed. "Thank you! What is it?" she asked.

"Open it! Open it!" Ann Polanski urged, and we gasped when she did. It was a box full of pastries. "My mother made these." We just stood wide-eyed, gaping. "They are to be eaten. Let's all have some!" She produced some stiff paper napkins from her bag, and we tasted cakes and tarts we had forgotten existed. She kept urging us to eat more and then closed the box. "For the train. They should taste good," she said.

"Thank you, thank you!" we shouted.

"Tell your mother she's a superb cook!" Vitya said.

"You are all welcome; my mother will be glad you enjoyed her pastries so much." She smiled.

"Now for business. You know that you are to sail from Antwerp, Belgium. Six tickets on the *Kronland* will be waiting for you when you get there. All arrangements have been made. The steamship company will arrange the dates for your sailing. You have passports, visas. I can't think of another thing and see no reason why you can't leave tomorrow," she said.

We cheered and hugged each other, feeling as if we had just been released from chains. Ann Polanski clapped her hands in mock anger. "Well, will you leave or do you like it so well here that you want to stay? Remember, tram number fifteen will take you to the station. When you get there, buy tickets all the way to Antwerp, Belgium—it may be cheaper. . . ." She stopped. "You have enough money?" Lev felt for his money belt.

"We sold the last of our jewelry—I think we should have enough," he said. Ann Polanski looked at us seriously, as Mother used to do.

"I am happy that you are leaving, but also sad because I like you all." She bent down and kissed Sasha. Vera ran to her and hugged her. When she straightened up, she looked at us intensely. "What fine children you are!" she cried, and kissed me, Vitya, and Marina. When she extended her hand to Lev, he bowed and kissed it. "Goodbye, dear friends! Good luck! Write to me when you get to America." She was no sooner out of the door than Lev motioned us to come closer to him.

"Is there any reason why we can't leave right now?" he whispered.

Without a word, we started to pack the food we had left. We got our coats and held our noses against the stench as we walked down those putrid stairs for the final time.

It was sunny, and the huge gray cobblestones looked like puddles of water and I began skipping over them until we reached the massive gate. Without looking back, we walked down the street to the tram stop.

28

WE SAT QUIETLY in the almost-empty tram, peering through dirty windows. After so many weeks in Warsaw, all we knew of the city was the prison-like cobblestone courtyard and our miserable living quarters. The stench of the building clung to our clothes, to our very beings, yet somehow I felt sad. We were again moving, farther away from Russia, and I realized that I felt homesick. Was someone now living in our cottage? Did Grisha get back all right? The faces of the Mieszkowskis came before me—how were they? Parazka—how and where was she? My mind flew from one thought to the other.

When we arrived at the station, Lev ordered us, "Stay right here. I'm going to get tickets and it may take a little time." His voice drifted off with him and we waited in silence. Not one of us showed any feeling of excitement or elation. We had so looked forward to getting out of Warsaw, to being on our way to America, yet here we stood in silence, not a joyous feeling among us.

Lev looked wretched when he came back. "What's wrong? What's happened?" Marina cried. He lifted his arms in a gesture of despair.

"I had no idea how expensive these trains are." He pulled a slip of paper out of his pocket. "Warsaw is very far from Antwerp. We simply haven't enough money to take us all the way there." He held out some orange slips. "Here they are, tickets to Berlin only—I spent all the money we had!"

Seeing how unhappy he was, Marina cried, "That's not bad; let's get started; we'll manage!" Lev looked at her gratefully.

"We'll simply have to manage!" He tried to smile.

Once again trains and railway stations became part of our very existence. We were too tired and anxious even to look out at the scenery as the train flew past. We had but one thought—Berlin. When the train stopped in a small town and we were asked to get off, Lev became hysterical.

"We have tickets, passports to Berlin," he pleaded.

"This is the end. Now we turn around and go back to Warsaw," the conductor said.

"But Berlin," Lev cried.

"Ah, your Berlin train will be in soon. Stay here." He watched us descend onto the platform and shouted, "Good luck!" He had no idea how we needed it! Two hours later, our passports and tickets stamped, we were on the train to Berlin. It was the best train we had ever been on, and we enjoyed the comfortable seats and slept until a loud voice close to us shouted, "Berlin in twenty minutes."

We dashed to the restrooms, washed as best we could, and were ready minutes before our train arrived.

At the station we were amazed to see the many shops, food stalls, and restaurants. At one place we stopped and watched a bread-cutting machine! Amazing. A whole long loaf of bread sliced in seconds! Under the machine, there was a paper sack to catch the crumbs. The hands of the man cutting the bread moved fast, tossing the crusts into the same bag. We watched hungrily.

"Can I go and ask him if we could have the crumbs and the end pieces?" Vera begged.

"Very well," said Lev. "Watch for a while, and when the bread cutter is not too busy, ask if you can have them." We started walking away, and Lev suddenly shouted, "You don't talk German—how will you ask him?"

"Leave it to Vera—she'll find a way to ask or the man will offer them to her when he sees her," Vitya said.

Vitya was right. We watched Vera from a distance. She stood on tiptoe, her eyes on the bread cutter and his partner, who grabbed the bread and made sandwiches. They both worked very fast and there was always someone waiting for a made-up sandwich, or for a sliced loaf of bread.

"Vera must have lost her nerve," Lev said. "She's been there quite a while." He no sooner finished talking than we saw Vera running toward us, a large bag in her hands.

"I got it; I got it!" she cried happily, and we started looking for a place to sit down.

Marina looked into the bag. "Enough crumbs and crusts for a good breakfast—let's hope there's some hot water!" She started for the rest room. "Get washed! Good hot water!" She handed the cup to me. Though we did not divide the contents in the bag, we helped ourselves, mindful of the number of us who had to be fed. Surprisingly enough, there were more crusts and crumbs than we anticipated, and passing around the cup of hot water, which was refilled when it was empty, we had enough to eat.

Our hunger appeased somewhat, we were thinking of our next step, how we could possibly continue our trip without any money when Sasha cried, "Why don't we tell the conductor that someone stole our tickets?" We laughed.

"I wish we could do that," Lev said, "but even if we don't have money, I'm going to the ticket window to see when the trains leave, if there is a train straight to Antwerp."

"Is it very far from Berlin?" Vitya asked.

"I don't know, but it's too far to walk!" Lev said sadly as he went away.

We sat quietly for a long time until Lev returned. "There is a direct train to Antwerp tomorrow."

Marina watched him as he spoke and unexpectedly burst into tears. "Here we talk of taking trains and we haven't a penny among us."

Lev looked down at his worn shoes. "You're right; we are in real trouble," he said.

"No!" Vitya cried. "We will get on the train as if we had tickets. We will be thrown off at the next stop, but then we will get on the next train, and that way get closer and closer to the place we want to go."

"I think Vitya is right," Lev said. "I know that some people have done it—I think we must try it! We can even hide in freight wagons—let's do it!" Marina, who had been so discouraged at first, sounded more cheerful.

"I'm all for taking the chance," she said.

"Good, then we'll plan to leave for Belgium tomorrow," he said. We nodded and felt better. We had made a decision. It had to work!

Again, with one of us always watching our place, we wandered around the station, looking at people, listening to the language, which was not familiar, and looking in shop windows. My mouth watered as I stood before the window of a large restaurant, my eyes glued to the food people were eating. I kept imagining what it would be like to walk in and order a meal. What would I choose if I could have anything I wanted? My eyes traveled from table to table, trying to see what foods people had chosen, and my gaze met the deep blue eyes of an old gentleman. His almost-gray hair was longer than that of most men, and his equally gray wide beard strongly reminded me of someone I knew. We had been looking at each other for fully a minute before I realized that he was motioning me to come in. Hesitantly, I opened the door, expecting someone to tell me to get out, but the gentleman came toward me and saved me from the red-faced waiter who was ready to do just that.

"*Komm.*" He led me to his table and held the chair for me to sit down. "*Bist du hungrig?*" he asked softly, his large eyes searching my face. I didn't speak German but knew what he meant. I lowered my eyes and looked at the table. He pushed his almost-full plate of food toward me. "*Isst du, isst du, mein kind,*" he urged. I understood, and quickly grabbing the roll he handed me, started dipping pieces of it into the juices on the plate, stuffing them into my mouth. Some small bones with bits of meat clinging to them were soon in my dirty fingers. I was licking, biting, chewing as fast as I could until I had licked them clean. He watched me silently, a pained expression on his face. "*Fertig?*" he asked, handing me a roll wrapped in a large paper napkin. He pushed his chair back and put on his black overcoat, and I watched him, trying to understand my strong feeling that somehow I knew this man.

"*Danke,*" I finally said, using one of the few German words I knew. When he smiled, suddenly I knew exactly who he was. I had seen his face on the covers of Mama's music, the music we had played at home. *"Herr Brahms!"* I cried ecstatically. He grinned, followed me out the door, pushed something into my hand, and walked away slowly, just the way I would have expected Brahms to do!

I ran back to our place and found Lev sitting alone. "Look!" I cried, pushing the paper I had in my hand into his. He unfolded it carefully.

"My God! Twenty-five thousand marks. Where did you get it?" He sounded frightened. I told them about my meeting with Mr. Brahms.

"How do you know his name? Did he tell you he was Brahms?" Lev asked.

"He did not have to tell me. There were enough pictures of him on our music," I explained. "Actually, he is even more handsome than his pictures. His face is so kind!" Lev burst out laughing.

"Olya, Johannes Brahms who wrote music has been dead for many years, but—" he fingered the paper bill in his hand—"it is a miracle, a real miracle, whatever his name is."

When the others came back Lev told him about my Mr. Brahms and showed them the money.

"How wonderful!" Marina cried.

"Every penny of this goes for the train fare—as far as it will take us, perhaps even to Antwerp," said Lev emphatically. "I'm going to the ticket office right away."

He came back with tickets that would take us as far as Düsseldorf on the Antwerp train, which he had discovered would leave at five in the morning. Now I mentally blessed Mr. Brahms for filling my belly so graciously, and when we stretched out on the cluttered wooden floor, I slept, heedless of the chugging engines and the clamoring din of people.

It was still dark when we boarded the train, but while we were finding and settling ourselves in our seats, the black of night was changing to deep gray, growing lighter and lighter. It was morning. Sleep clung to us, but hunger was more aggressive. There was increased stirring and movement. Passengers who had been traveling all night were stretching, going to the washrooms, and we marveled at seeing them return so miraculously clean and refreshed. When they started to open parcels of food, Lev tried to keep us from staring, but it was impossible. Our eyes refused to look elsewhere. We could almost taste the cheeses, meats, hard-boiled eggs, and buttered rolls.

Seeing our hungry faces, an old gentleman and his wife gave us the remains of their food when they got off the train.

Marina opened the bag. "God is really looking after us!" she cried. There were thick slices of bread, rolls, ham, and hard-boiled eggs. It was as if a spring within us snapped, freeing us from a constraint which hurt from head to toe. We ate and ate and cleaned the bag of every scrap. It was so wonderful not to be hungry. Hunger attacks the body and mind. Both belong to hunger. What started out to be a miserable empty day turned out to be a beautiful one because of two generous, sensitive people.

When the train started up again, Lev fearfully held up his tickets. The conductor punched them and handed them back to Lev. "You have a long way to go to get to Düsseldorf."

"I wish we had a map or knew more geography," Marina said. "Where is Düsseldorf? Is it in Belgium?" She knit her brows.

"We'll know when guards come on to ask for our passports," Lev said. Now, instead of hunger, our great concern was distance. Düsseldorf! How much longer could we remain on the train? By late afternoon, we decided to ask the conductor.

"*Wann kommen wir Düsseldorf an?*" Lev asked. The conductor looked at his watch.

"*Eine Stunde vierzig Minuten,*" he said. We understood his reply. A pronouncement of doom for us. Vitya was thoughtful for a few minutes.

"Listen," she finally said. "This train goes to Belgium and we're not going to get off!"

"Are you mad? Would you rather we were put off in some small village and arrested?" Lev asked. Vitya's chin was jutting out as it always did when she was particularly determined.

"I have an idea. Can we discuss it and take a vote?" she said.

"I know what your idea is—it's madness!" Lev cried.

Marina looked at him with annoyance. "Don't you think she should be allowed to explain it? Go on, Vitya," she said. Vitya needed no coaxing.

"We know that there are compartments carrying people's luggage and other heavy goods—"

"What has that to do with us?" Marina interrupted her.

"Let me finish!" Vitya was impatient and continued. "Long before we get to Düsseldorf we should walk from carriage to carriage from the front to the back until we find one, and hide there. Tickets aren't collected—we could get off in Belgium," she said. There was a long silence.

"Scary like when we were in Grisha's wagon!" Sasha cried.

"Yes, but just as important to be quiet, especially when

we hear someone in that carriage moving suitcases," Vitya told him.

"Actually not a bad idea, Vitya," said Lev, "but it is so cold, and even in our coats, bundled up close together, we might be like frozen ducks when we got to Belgium. We must think of a better way."

"I think what Vitya says makes sense." Marina seemed excited at the prospect. "How about it, Olya? Vera?" she asked.

"I'm with you," I cried.

"Me, too!" Vera and Sasha said excitedly.

"You have all the votes, Vitya; let's investigate," Lev said. "You go through the carriages up front. I'll do the same going backward."

Without another word both left their seats and started on their mission. Marina asked Vera and Sasha to use the rest rooms.

"Come," she said. "I'll go with you." When we returned, Lev and Vitya were just coming back.

"There's a carriage full of luggage next to this one, and you're right, it is cold," Vitya said.

"I found one about four along," Lev said. "Which should we choose?"

"Don't you think the one up front close to this one would be better?" Marina asked. "We might even be able to sneak back to use the rest rooms."

"Next one along it is. We must be nonchalant so we don't arouse the conductor's suspicion!" Vitya warned.

"Should we all go together?" Marina asked.

"Yes," Lev answered, "we mustn't be separated."

"Let's stop in the rest room," Vitya said, "and from there we go right to our hiding place."

Tensely, we followed Lev through the door left open

by the conductor and were in the next carriage. The door to the luggage compartment was harder to open, but Lev managed it, and we found ourselves in total darkness and had to grope our way, holding on to boxes and suitcases.

"If we could squeeze into the middle of these boxes, it might be warmer and we could lean against them," Vitya whispered.

We stood in place while Lev and Vitya pushed various things aside, and finally Lev said, "Take my hand and I'll tell you where to sit." The iron floor was very cold. It was still daylight, but the only light we had came from the wide cracks in the locked doors in the middle of the car. We sat huddled together, our coats buttoned, but the cold swiftly penetrated through our clothes.

"We're on our way!" Vitya whispered through chattering teeth, trying to sound cheerful. Sitting on the iron floor so close to the wheels, we felt the rocking, swaying movement accompanied by noises we never knew trains ever made, and their effect on us was not good. We felt dizzy and sleepy and were grateful that sleep overcame us. We had no idea how long we slept, and I didn't want to wake up, but a persistent sound close to me forced me to open my eyes. Vera! Vera was crying piteously and I heard Marina's voice pleading with her to be quiet. I sat up, suddenly bumping my head against something.

"What's the matter with Vera?" I asked above the loud rhythmic *chug-a-chug-chug-chug* of the wheels flying over the rails. Marina did not answer me. "It's Vera—her toes hurt—she cried like this in the bakery!" I shouted.

"Sh-sh!" Lev said miserably.

"Aren't you going to get her out of here?" I was angry.

"We are trying to go as far as we possibly can. Maybe we'll get off at the next stop," Marina whispered.

There were voices on the other side of the door. We must have been heard because the door suddenly opened. We held our breaths. We could not see anyone but knew that one or more people had come in. Someone lit a lantern. There were two men and both were looking at a paper. "These are the boxes to be taken off at the next stop. I'll call the number and when you see it on a box, push it forward to be taken off the train."

They had not discovered us! Vitya held her hand over Vera's mouth. The rest of us hardly dared breathe. The men moved slowly, their heavy boots striking the iron floors. "Two boxes more," one of them said, and our hearts almost stopped beating as they came close to those surrounding us. Suddenly, one of them lifted the lantern high above our heads.

"*Gott im Himmel*—stowaways," he shouted. We were close to the door leading to the next carriage, and Lev, grabbing Vera in his arms, began pushing a huge box blocking our way out from the maze of boxes to the door. As one man grabbed him, the other shouted, "Boxes first—they must come off. We'll get the *Kinder* later—they can't go very far!"

We all squeezed through the small opening between the boxes and reached the door, opened it quickly, and found ourselves in a carriage very different from the one we had been riding in before.

We were in a long, carpeted corridor with doors on one side. Undecided, frightened, we stood momentarily, wondering what to do, when the door from the luggage compartment opened and one of the men shouted, "Here they are! Get the conductor." Without thinking or knowing where it would lead to, we opened the first door and dashed in. It was a small room, wonderfully warm, softly lit. We stood, breathless, shaking with fright, when a tall man, whom we had not noticed because he was sitting in the shadow by the window, suddenly stood up before us. He put out his arms and reached for Vera, who began to sob.

"Don't let him take me; I'll be good!"

"Don't be frightened." The man patted her. "I won't let anyone hurt you," he told her. He put her gently on a sofa bed at one end of the room, covered her carefully, and turned to us.

"*Qu'est-ce qu'il y a?*" His voice was gentle and his large blue eyes were full of sympathy. We were too shaken to answer, and when we stopped shaking, Lev spoke.

"We must get to Antwerp, but our tickets are good only as far as Düsseldorf. We hoped to remain hidden, but . . ." Lev stopped and pointed to Vera, who was still moaning softly. "Vera's feet were frozen once and she suffers from severe cold—we were discovered." His voice broke and he stopped. The man shook his head sadly.

"So many hardships for you all who are so young!" he said and started moving things about. "It's not a big room, but we should manage to sit down," he said, pointing to places for us.

"But the conductor—the other men will come soon—we'll be put off at the next stop; maybe we'll be arrested," said Vitya. The man looked at us.

"You poor children! All the troubles you have had—but don't worry about the conductor. I'll take care of the tickets or whatever is necessary. Let's make ourselves as comfortable as possible, squeezed in such small quarters. Let's talk. You speak French well—but you are Russian, aren't you?" Lev looked uneasy and the tall dark man smiled again. "You have no reason to be afraid of me. I promise to get you to . . ." He stopped. "I'm going as far as Brussels—

not at all far from Antwerp," he said. Lev looked at us and his eyes seemed to ask, "Can we trust him?" We looked at the man on the sofa near Vera. He was neither old nor young, and like Papa his dark mustache was mixed with gray. We liked him, especially his eyes.

"Yes, we are Russian," Lev said, "and things have not been going well for us."

"Your saving us now is about the most wonderful thing to happen to us—thank you!" Vitya added shyly. His face turned very serious.

"There is much suffering and pain in this world. All I can do is try and be a decent human being. I am only a professor at the University in Brussels. I have no power or influence. I am happy to help a little." He stopped and suddenly said, "My name is Benois, Pierre Benois—and you must be starved! All I have is some fruit and a box of chocolates. This—" he held up a box—"it was to have been for my girls, three of them, but they won't miss it when I tell them about you."

We were enjoying the fruit and chocolates immensely when a knock on the door brought us all to our feet. Professor Benois motioned for us to sit as we were and opened the door. It was the conductor with the two men from the luggage compartment.

"Sorry to disturb you, sir," said the conductor. "We are looking for some stowaways," and, seeing us seated, stared open-mouthed. "Those are the stowaways! They must be dealt with properly," he shouted angrily.

"That won't be necessary!" Professor Benois calmly replied as he took a wallet from his pocket. "How much are tickets from here to Brussels?" The conductor took the money and handed him the tickets.

"*Schön, mein Herr.*"

"*Danke*," he said as he closed the door.

The relief of feeling safe, the warmth, and the wonderful chocolates made us drowsy, and we slept unashamedly. We could not remember when we had been this comfortable! When Professor Benois woke us, we were sure we had been dreaming, but it certainly was not a dream. One by one, we used the tiny bathroom of the compartment, trying to get some of the dirt off, but nothing helped. We still looked dirty and grubby.

"I'm sorry we look so awful!" Marina said. "We escaped with only the clothes we had on."

Professor Benois sighed. "So unfair for young children like yourselves to be faced with so many difficulties," he said. "We'll try and help."

Soon Professor Benois started gathering his belongings and put on his black cape, and we knew we were to get off the train with him. The same conductor who had chased and screamed at us now helped us off, and we followed Professor Benois into the waiting room.

"I must get home to my family, but will take you into this restaurant. After you have had a good breakfast, you will sit here and wait for someone to get you." He spoke to a lady who was seating people and gave her some bills. "I must go. Here's my card. I will not be back for you, but I promise someone will come for you and start you on your way for your boat to America." He kissed Vera, Sasha, and me, and the hands of Vitya and Marina. When he shook hands with Lev, he said, "Have no fears. You will be picked up even though you may have to wait here till lunchtime." He smiled, waved, and walked out. He and his long cape were soon enveloped by the large crowds in the station.

29

THE HOSTESS SEATED us at a large table and disappeared. "What if no one comes for us?" Vitya asked.

"Surely we can trust Professor Benois," Lev answered. "He's a good man. We even have his card." Lev sounded indignant, but all the same, Vitya had planted a seed of doubt in us which made us uneasy. We looked at the large menus in French and marveled at the selections.

"I didn't think there was so much food left in the whole world!" Marina said. "Can we choose what we want or do you suppose Professor Benois paid for just bread and tea?" she asked, her eyes glued to the menu.

"We must not order too much to run up a big bill for the professor," Marina said when the waiter stopped at our table. "Tea and bread for us all," Marina said in French.

The waiter was startled. "I was told that you may all order anything you wish." He looked puzzled.

"Oh," Marina said. "We may order anything we want,"

she told us. Happily we ordered a breakfast like none we had had in a long, long time and ate ravenously.

"I wonder what he thinks." Marina looked toward the waiter. "Our being so dirty and unkempt, yet ordering such an elegant breakfast."

"I wouldn't worry what he thinks; let's enjoy our good food!" Lev said.

We had not even finished our croissants and hot chocolate when two well-dressed women, one large and the other very young, pretty, and blond, stopped at our table. Lev rose from his chair but said nothing. The women looked at each of us carefully.

"You are the Koshanskys?" one asked pleasantly.

"And you must be the people Professor Benois said would come to meet us and tell us about getting to Antwerp!" Lev cried happily.

"Yes, I am Marie Benois, his mother, and this is his oldest daughter, my granddaughter, Madeleine." We smiled at them, so grateful that they had come.

"Your son is the most wonderful man, and you are equally splendid to come to our help," Marina told her.

"My son is wonderful. I'll accept that readily," she said, dimpling, and we realized that despite her bulky frame, her face was beautiful, and we saw that Professor Benois had his mother's soft, gentle blue eyes. Her graying hair swept up into a neat knot was held secure by heavy hairpins. There was a faint smell of cologne we enjoyed, but most of all, we were impressed by her hands. They were white, delicate, soft, and beautiful. We wished we could sit on ours, hide them so that she might not see them. Madame Benois sensed our embarrassment.

"I know only too well how hard it is to look fresh while traveling," she said sympathetically.

"It looks as if we'll have to wait until we are on the boat to America before we can have a thorough scrubbing," said Marina. "The most important thing now is for us to get to Antwerp and to our ship to America," she added.

Madame Benois again looked at us closely. "There are some things you should understand before you make definite decisions." Our hearts sank.

Madame Benois told us that we would not be allowed to board the ship until we had been examined by doctors. Many people, rejected as unwell, were forced to wait for long periods. It had been arranged with the HIAS office for us to stay in Brussels so that we could rest and get ourselves and our clothes clean.

Madame Benois took us in her carriage to a large yellow stone house where we were to live for a few days. There Mademoiselle Gabrielle ushered us in, and we followed her up a long flight of stairs. She walked ahead silently and then pointed to a room.

"For the girls," she said and motioned us to follow her in. "Your brothers will be next door!" she said and left us. We looked around. It wasn't a large room. The two double beds were close to each other, and the large white bureau had a strange-shaped mirror above it. We stood before it and stared momentarily at our images.

"God, we look awful," Marina said.

"Maybe we'll look even worse when we leave," Vitya said angrily, but Marina pretended not to hear her. A large wooden clothes cabinet was empty. "I wonder what's in store for us next?" Vitya asked and sat down on one of the beds.

"It feels good. Maybe she'll make us take a nap!" Marina said. It somehow sounded funny and we laughed.

"I wish I knew what was going to happen!" Vitya sounded worried.

There was a soft knock on the door and Mademoiselle Gabrielle, followed by an enormously tall woman, their hands full of cans and bottles, came into the room. We were frightened. *What now?* we wondered, but we hadn't much time to think.

"Take your clothes off!" Mademoiselle Gabrielle said, and we moved closer in panic. Vitya started for the door, but it wouldn't open, and she came back and we moved even closer to each other, rigid and frightened. Mademoiselle Gabrielle's voice softened. "You poor dears, don't be afraid. You must take your clothes off so that we can help rid you of the lice in your hair and bodies," she said.

"Lice?" Marina was indignant.

"Yes, lice!" Mademoiselle Gabrielle repeated. "And it is no wonder. You have been wearing these clothes for so long! When was your hair washed last?" she asked. We hung our heads. We knew we were dirty, but to have someone tell us this was humiliating.

"There was no place where we could wash our hair and we have no other clothes!" Vitya cried. The tall woman looked at us sympathetically.

"I'm Françoise. Don't be afraid." Her voice was kind and gentle. Vera went up to her. Françoise unbuttoned Vera's dress, took off all her clothes, and there she stood naked.

"I want to be clean! Even my belly button is dirty!" she cried. Françoise and Mademoiselle Gabrielle laughed.

"We are used to this. Please don't be embarrassed," Mademoiselle Gabrielle said.

It was strange to be in a room, naked, with two strangers in heavy aprons and rubber gloves massaging our heads with

liquids smelling like paraffin and similar horrible smells.
"Put these on." Mademoiselle Gabrielle handed us
roomy, long white robes. "Bath now," she said and she and
Françoise led us through the corridor and stopped before
a door. *"Salle de bains,"* Mademoiselle Gabrielle said.

It certainly was different from any other bathroom we
had ever seen. On one side of the wall, there were cubicles
with a toilet in each. There were the same number of
cubicles on the opposite side of the room with nothing in
them.

"Where is the bath?" Vitya asked. There was none in
sight. Mademoiselle Gabrielle smiled, and Françoise reached
up and moved a handle and immediately there came a large
straight stream of water. We moved back cautiously, staring
in surprise.

"Go on in. It will feel good!" Mademoiselle Gabrielle
urged, and we cautiously put our hands under the water
first, and within seconds the warm water was coming down
over our heads and bodies and Françoise and Mademoiselle
Gabrielle were scrubbing us as if we were infants! It was
wonderful to feel the warm water over us. We dried ourselves with thick white towels and returned to our room.

"How long must we stay like this?" Vitya asked.

"As long as it takes to get rid of the lice you have
collected over the last months," Mademoiselle Gabrielle
said.

"May we get dressed?" Marina asked. Françoise looked
at her and began piling our clothes into a large canvas bag
as if each piece was a deadly diseased object.

"Don't do that! We have no other clothes." Marina
ran to her.

"There will be other clothes for you," Françoise said.
"As soon as I have cleared up, I'll bring lunch."

To our happy surprise, Lev and Sasha walked in with her when she reappeared in our room with a basket of food. Their heads, too, were wrapped in towels. Sasha ran to us as if he hadn't seen us for weeks.

Lev burst out laughing. "We look like—we look like—"

"Turks?" Marina asked. "I think they wear things on their heads," she cried.

"But we are clean, and Sasha and I have haircuts!" Lev told us. "The worst is over."

We were surprisingly hungry after such a good breakfast a short while before, and Françoise asked us if we wanted more rolls or milk. Imagine being offered more milk! We drank it slowly, carefully, tasting the smoothness. It reminded us of Parazka-days in our big house when Mama and Parazka urged us to drink milk! We were embarrassed to eat so much, but Françoise did not seem surprised at our food consumption.

"Anything else I can get you?" she asked as she stood at the door.

"We'd love some books or newspapers," Lev told her. Françoise soon returned with several French newspapers. We thanked her and each took one section to see what we could learn from an old newspaper in the French language, and settled on one of our beds. Sasha and Vera were again playing cat's cradle. The room was quiet, we were well fed, content, when suddenly there came a scream from Lev. His fists clenched, he kept mumbling over and over again:

"Killed, they killed them all! They killed the whole family, all of them! Damn their souls!"

"Who, Lev—who was killed?" Marina cried. Lev looked at her, shaking his head.

"Tsar Nicholas, and all his family, shot down like vicious animals—all the Romanovs, the very last of them!"

"When did it happen?" Marina cried. Lev looked at the date of the paper.

"About three months ago. We were still in Russia!" he said. "Banishing them, taking away their power would have been enough, but killing off the whole family—it is monstrous!" he cried angrily.

When Mademoiselle Gabrielle came in, she looked at us, puzzled. *"Qu'y a-t-il?"* she asked.

"Rien," Lev said, and she knew that whatever it was that troubled him or the rest of us, we were not going to tell her.

Lev and Sasha returned to their room just as Françoise came in with toothbrushes and toothpaste. The last time we had used them was on the night before we left our big house. Mama was so sure she had packed them, including extras, but we never found them and we had not brushed our teeth since. What luxury! Clean nightgowns, toothbrushes and the wonderful smell of toothpaste! We climbed into bed, Vera and I in one, Marina and Vitya in the other.

"Don't remove the towels from your heads," Françoise warned. We were asleep by the time she had put out the lights and said good night.

It took another day of head massage and hair-washing before we were free of lice. Then our hair shone clean in the sunlight and we could not stop admiring ourselves.

"Now for clothes." Mademoiselle Gabrielle was opening boxes. "Underwear, two sets of each," she said. Then she gave each of us a three-piece suit consisting of a skirt, blouse, and jacket. They were different colors, but all the same style.

"Discontinued school uniforms," Françoise said admiringly, but Mademoiselle Gabrielle gave her a sharp look of disapproval. Françoise was soon busy helping us button skirts and blouses.

"These—" Mademoiselle pointed to some clothes in the wooden clothes cupboard— "you are to take with you." She suddenly stopped. "You certainly look different! No one will know you—wait until Madame Benois sees you!" She smiled.

"These are beautiful clothes, just beautiful." We beamed, thanking Mademoiselle Gabrielle. Mademoiselle Gabrielle smiled and picked up two more large boxes.

"I almost forgot; coats, gloves, and berets. It is winter!" she said, looking at our feet. "Your old shoes—we could do nothing about shoes!"

When Lev and Sasha came to our room, we were overwhelmed. Lev looked thin, but so much taller! His navy suit fitted him well and we wondered who had tied the necktie for him. Sasha, too, looked so different. His knees were showing, between the top of his gray wool socks and short trousers. He had a sweater under his gray jacket. They both looked so handsome! How happy Mama would have been to see us clean and well dressed! My mind turned to Papa. Would he be pleased with us?

Madame Benois hardly recognized us. "I had no idea what handsome children you are," she said when she arrived, and Vera and I curtsied as Vitya and Marina had done. It was a spontaneous reaction to her compliment and our way of greeting older people when we lived in our big white house, or when Papa and Mama presented us to friends.

"It's a lovely day," Madame Benois said. "I've come to fetch you to my son's home. He has some good news for you!" She sounded as young and excited as the rest of us.

"Can you tell us the news? Please do!" Lev begged. Madame Benois laughed.

"I wouldn't know where to begin—come, my son and the girls are waiting for us. Come."

30

ONCE AGAIN WE rode along the beautiful wide avenue that we had so enjoyed when Madame Benois first took us to the HIAS. However, this time her effort in pointing out places of particular interest was wasted on us. Our minds were only on seeing the professor. We so wanted to hear the news he had for us.

"Wouldn't it be wonderful if he had word for us from Papa?" Lev whispered. We smiled wistfully. Papa was the horizon we were trying to reach, but there was a heavy curtain between us. Grisha was the first to penetrate this curtain. Then it was the HIAS. We ourselves had not had direct word from Papa since the first letter arrived for Mother. Now it seemed as if the HIAS had become Papa.

The carriage stopped outside a modest tall yellow stone house, four stories high, with brightly painted shutters and wide steps. As we reached the steps, the door flew open and Madeleine cried, "Hurry, hurry, *Grand-mère!*" We rushed up the stairs and through the wide green door and found ourselves in a large living room. Madeleine shyly hugged us. Professor Benois introduced us to his delicate, very blond wife, seated in a large chair before a fireplace, and to his two younger daughters, whom we had not met before. The girls had their mother's delicate features, blond hair and pink complexions, and were as outgoing and talkative as their grandmother.

By the time lunch was ready, we had decided that Professor Benois would tell us his news when he was ready. We watched him walk up to his wife and were surprised to see him push her chair toward the dining room and realized it was a wheelchair. He guided it carefully to the head of the table, where she looked delicately beautiful in the sun-filled room.

"I hope you are all hungry," young Madame Benois said. "*Grand-mère* sent her fine cook to prepare our lunch and her feelings would be hurt if we didn't eat a lot!"

"Professor Benois knows quite well how much we can eat!" Marina said, looking at him.

"Just be sure we do justice to my cook's lunch," *Grand-mère* said with a twinkle in her eye.

After lunch Professor Benois asked us to come into his study, and all but Vera and Sasha followed him eagerly.

"Have you heard from my father—telegram—what?" Lev asked anxiously as soon as we were seated.

"No, I have not had the pleasure of having any contact with your father, but I hope to some day." Seeing our unhappy faces, the professor added, "Don't worry. My mother and I have worked out all the details through the HIAS office, which is most efficient. You sail tomorrow at five," he said happily. His news made no impression on us.

"What's wrong?" He looked at each of our faces carefully.

"We cannot understand it. Not one word to us from my father," Vitya cried. "There must be some good reason, but I'm beginning to wonder if he wants us."

Professor Benois jumped up from his chair. "Of course he wants you, you dear silly children. He is paying for your trip, which is very costly. There must be some good reason for his silence. Tomorrow at this time you will be on your way and what a reunion it will be!" He started to look in his pockets and produced an envelope. "My mother gave this to me for you. You will need a little money for one thing or another." He handed the envelope to Lev.

Lev looked at the heavy handwriting and read out loud, " 'For my good friends, the Koshanskys.' This will enable us to buy food!" he shouted gleefully.

Professor Benois laughed. "Lev, on board ship, food is supplied. This money is for extras. You may want to buy chocolate or some other things."

Marina put her hands over her face. "How can we ever thank you and your dear family for all you have done for us?"

"We might still be stranded in some small town in Germany if it weren't for you," Vitya said.

"Your father would have done the same if my children had been in trouble," he said.

The next morning we all got into two carriages with Madame Benois and the girls and set off for the station.

"Here's our train. Right on time!" Madame Benois announced and counted us like small children as we walked up the platform and into our large compartment. There were seats for us all, and the trip to Antwerp, which took only a little over an hour, was too short. We were having such a good time talking, singing, and teasing, and we were sorry the train trip was over.

"Now for lunch." Madame Benois led us into a spacious restaurant.

Our hands washed and clothes straightened, we were glad to sit down. We were also hungry and when the hot mushroom soup arrived, we ate ravenously.

"I don't advise rolls. Save room for the next courses," Madame Benois cautioned. The main dish was an egg-and-cheese quiche, something we had never tasted before. Dessert, strawberries with a white, fluffy top, tasted wonderful. The Benois watched us with more than just a hint of amusement. We had never tasted whipped cream.

"Heavens!" Madame Benois suddenly said. "It is later than I thought, time to get you to your ship." She opened her large purse and took out a thick envelope. "These are your tickets." She handed them to Lev. "Everything is taken care of. You are expected on the *Kronland*."

"The what?" Marina sounded frightened.

Madame Benois laughed. "The *Kronland*, the ship to take you to New York," she said.

Marina blushed. "I did know and should have remembered," she said.

"You have had too much to remember, too many responsibilities, but now, after you are examined by the medical staff, there are no more problems. You are healthy and clean." Madame Benois grinned at us.

"We have you to thank for that," Lev said.

When we left the restaurant and squeezed into one large carriage, no one spoke. Even Madeleine and Vitya were quiet as we drove to the docks. The Benois' silence, we hoped, was due to the fact that they would miss us.

Our silence was due to anxiety. Would Papa meet us or would someone come in his place?

"Smell the salt water?" Madame Benois asked. We sniffed the cold air and looked at the street, crowded with carriages and people carrying trunks and suitcases of every description. It grew more crowded as we neared the dock. The carriage stopped, Madame Benois got out, and the rest of us piled out after her. "You have your papers, everything you need; your suitcases will be delivered to your cabin." Lev nodded. "You know how to reach us if you want to write to us?" she asked. Marina nodded and threw her arms about Madame Benois. We all kissed her and the girls, quietly and tenderly, and then stood looking at each other.

"Go now," Madame Benois cried, shooing the girls back into the carriage. "Walk straight ahead. The gentlemen on either side of the road will direct you," she cried as the carriage drove off.

As if suddenly awakened from sleep, we realized we were at dock number sixty-one and that before us there was a huge ship, longer than any train we had ever seen. There were people everywhere. Tired-looking men and women, mothers with babies, older children holding on to their mothers' skirts. We joined the throngs and tried to listen to the multitude of languages surrounding us.

"Is that big house where we will live until we get to America?" Sasha cried, excitedly looking at the huge smokestacks. Lev laughed.

"It's a ship, Sasha, not a house," he said. We showed our tickets to a man in a green uniform, who directed us on board. We walked across a wooden bridge, the waves underneath lapping at the boards as if trying to get at our feet, hurried up some steep stairs, and were soon on the deck of the *Kronland* along with hundreds of other people. It was a big ship, as long as an elongated park, and we wondered how anything so big, with cargo and so many people, could stay afloat.

We pushed along with the crowd and had no idea where we were going until we saw a sign in many languages; EXAMINATIONS HERE. People stopped. Many spat on their palms to smooth their hair and squared their shoulders despite heavy luggage and unhappy weary children in their arms. From there we were taken separately to examining rooms, where doctors looked at our tongues, ears, throats, and hair. Gratefully, all of us passed the medical inspection, but we were sad to see many people rejected who had to leave the ship.

"Come, follow me." We heard a man's voice, and along with other fortunate beings like ourselves, we were led down several flights of steps. The more floors we walked down, the noisier it became; still we kept descending. When we reached what we thought was the very bottom of the ship, the man stopped. We were in a dimly lit hallway.

"This is your floor," he said, and started calling names, unlocking doors, and leaving the passengers in their cabins.

"Koshansky," he finally called, unlocking the door to our cabin. We looked into a pitch-black void. The man pushed a button on the wall, which gave us a dim light from the ceiling. "Meals are announced by a loud clanging bell. Just follow the crowd up several floors. Enjoy your crossing," he said.

We looked around the room. On each side there were three berths, or beds, one on top of the other with a blanket and pillow. A large towel rested at the foot of each bunk. There was not much else in the elongated small room.

"What do you think?" Lev looked at us. Vitya, having found a cupboard, was busy putting our things away. She turned to Lev.

"This is far better than sleeping on the floor in a railway station! We shouldn't complain. I think this room is just fine," she said, her chin jutting out, and we knew she was annoyed.

"So many people have been handling matters for Papa, maybe—maybe the person who made these arrangements for him just did not care," Marina said. "But I wish we had even a tiny window," she added. "Papa may not have any idea what arrangements are made for us."

"It doesn't matter!" Lev sounded angry. "Just choose which bunk you want to sleep in."

"Can we have the top beds?" Sasha and Vera asked at the same time.

"Of course!" Lev told them.

A loud knock on the door startled us. "Telegram for Lev Koshansky!" a voice called from the other side of the door, and Lev quickly opened it and took the envelope.

"Open it!" Vitya ordered more than asked, and we watched him tear the seal with trembling hands.

"It's from Papa!" cried Lev. He read, " 'Am counting days, hours, and minutes until I see my dear children. Will meet your ship in New York. All my love, Papa.' "

Lev folded the paper, but we reached and pulled it out of his hands. It was from Papa! Touching it was touching Papa, and our small windowless dark room, the bunks way up high, no longer mattered. Nothing mattered! We would soon be home with Papa!

FIC
POS

Posell, Elsa Z.

Homecoming.

$12.71

DATE DUE	BORROWER'S NAME	ROOM NO.
NO 27 '89	Kelly Klein	8
OCT 1 6 '91	Shannon Parrett	9th
	Jessica Godfrey	9th

FIC
POS

Posell, Elsa Z.

Homecoming.

**HIGH SCHOOL LIBRARY
STEPHENSON, MICHIGAN**